Matthew Kneale was born in London in 1960, the son of two writers. He studied at Oxford before spending a year in Tokyo where he taught English and first began writing. His latest book, *English Passengers*, was shortlisted for the 2000 Booker Prize and won the 2000 Whitbread Book of the Year Award. He travels extensively and has visited 83 countries and 7 continents to date.

Mr Foreigner

MATTHEW KNEALE

PHOENIX

To my parents

A PHOENIX PAPERBACK

First published in Great Britain in 1987
by Victor Gollancz Ltd as *Whore Banquets*
This edition published in 2002
by Weidenfeld & Nicolson

This paperback edition published in 2002
by Phoenix,
an imprint of Orion Books Ltd,
Orion House, 5 Upper St Martin's Lane,
London WC2H 9EA

A CIP catalogue record for this book
is available from the British Library.

ISBN 0 75381 306 8

Typeset at The Spartan Press Ltd,
Lymington, Hants

Printed and bound in Great Britain by
Clays Ltd, St Ives plc

Chapter One

Keiko Harada was wearing Mickey Mouse socks again. As she crossed her legs at the bar of the soup restaurant where they were eating, one of the Mickey Mice stared up at Daniel Thayne with a sinister gaze.

He was surprised by her moodiness. Conversation was a few sparse sentences between pauses, and when she spoke she would look away or past his head. Usually she was quiet, a little clinging.

The air conditioner spluttered twice, then resumed its drone. Daniel fished up a noodle with his chopsticks but it slipped back into the soup.

'Why are you wearing those socks?' he asked.

She raised the soup bowl to her lips – fat, sensual lips for a Japanese – and stared past his head. 'I like the Mickey Mouse. He live on my roof – I put him there.'

She meant that she had a Mickey Mouse poster on her bedroom ceiling. In the few months that he had known her, Daniel had become adept at deciphering her English. The better he understood her, the less he felt they had much to say to one another. Still he had let it go on.

'You hate it?' she asked, pouting her lips. Her face was round and slightly pinched, like a chipmunk's.

'Hate what?'

'The Mickey Mouse.'

He shook his head.

The slide door of the restaurant rattled open and in

came the sound of heavy rain, together with a draught of hot, damp air and a figure in military-style overalls and cap: a company worker searching for a late dinner. Catching sight of Daniel he looked quickly away, to mask his surprise at seeing a foreigner.

'I don't hate Mickey Mouse,' said Daniel. 'I just think it's strange that you wear his socks.'

She gave him a sharp look. 'Strange? What strange?'

'Just strange.' He wondered how he had caused offence with what had seemed such an innocent question.

'Maybe you think I am too told?' she demanded.

'Of course not,' he answered, trying to calm her. But he realized she was right – the socks were schoolgirl wear and looked odd on Keiko, a divorcee past thirty.

He dropped a handful of coins onto the bar and drained the last of his soup – a thin, salty liquid – leaving a brain-like residue of noodles at the bottom.

'Shall we go?'

Keiko slid off her bar-stool without a word. As they stepped outside into the dark, she clicked open her umbrella and held it above both their heads in a sudden, irked movement. Daniel took it from her – she was so tiny that she could barely hold it high enough.

They walked down a narrow lane lit with the signs of restaurants and bars, the downpour around them so strong that it ate up all the sounds except its own – the cars, the trains and the hum of the drinks machines were all gone. The rainy season had begun.

Daniel's senses took in the shapes and objects about him: the blurred glare of streetlights; the faint tappings of raindrops on his clothing. But he did not quite believe in them, or at least not in the way he would have believed in them in his own country. Before reaching Japan he had spent a year in Asia, wandering and taking photographs, easily enough time to pick up the mentality of a traveller. He had a sense of immunity from the events all around him, a confidence that they would not really affect him.

The lane widened and broke into two. Daniel turned towards the left.

'Wrong way,' announced Keiko crossly. 'More long.'

'No, let's go this way,' replied Daniel. 'It's quieter.'

With sour obedience Keiko turned to the left.

The other route passed a police box. Since his arrival in the country Daniel had felt a wariness towards the police, as he had been teaching English without a work permit. During the last few days this wariness had considerably increased, because he had lost his passport.

All foreigners were required to carry proof of identity by an obscure security law. For years this had been a dead letter, until a minor spy scandal had pushed the government into ordering random checks. A few unlucky westerners had even been imprisoned for an hour or two until their irate claims had been verified. Daniel's worry was that if he were caught he might be investigated and found to be working illegally. In such a case he would be quickly deported, penniless, to Korea or Hong Kong.

It was a danger he was well aware of. But still he did not fully believe it could affect him. He was separate.

The lane twisted amongst the rickety wood-frame buildings, then turned into a main road flanked by the empty, airfield-like expanse of a driving school. A gust of wind whisked rain beneath the umbrella and into their faces. Looking up, Daniel saw a thin figure walking towards them. From the slight stoop, the walk that needed a stick, he recognized Samuel Echtbein, the only other foreigner living in Takasago district. He was barely distinguishable as a westerner — his hair was closely cropped in the Japanese style, while his eyes were concealed behind thick glasses.

Drawing closer, he recognized Daniel and glanced with curiosity at Keiko. 'How're you doing?' he asked.

'Fine thanks,' said Daniel briefly; he saw the prying look in Echtbein's eyes and was unwilling to be drawn into conversation.

'You never told me about your girlfriend,' said Echtbein with a thin smile. 'Wanted to keep her secret from me, huh?'

'This is Keiko. Keiko, this is Samuel,' said Daniel reluctantly. She gave the newcomer a quick, polite nod.

'Nice to meet you Keiko.'

Daniel took a small sideways step, so he could get past Echtbein. 'We'd better be on our way – get out of the rain.'

'Sure. Well you must both drop in some time and meet my family.'

'Yes, that'd be great.' Daniel took another step away.

'Make it soon, huh?' Echtbein gave a minute laugh. 'Or else I'll have to come and drop in on you – check how you're both doing.'

Daniel managed an artificial chuckle and walked on, Keiko just beside him.

'He is your friend?' she demanded when they were out of earshot.

'No, just someone I've met a few times.'

'But why is he so much interest in you?'

'Who knows? Perhaps he has a soft spot for the English.'

Past a petrol pump they left the main road, slipping along an alley between two houses. A wooden stairway, each board bending beneath their steps, led to Keiko's flat. She briskly unlocked the flimsy door and walked into the steaminess beyond.

Except for the animals it was much like any other flat in Tokyo. Too small to contain much furniture, the claustrophobic size of the rooms was balanced by a rigid tidiness.

There was a mixture of styles. The bedroom was fully western, with carpet on the floor as well as a raised double bed. The sitting-room was more traditional, with tatami rush mats covering the ground and a low table that was surrounded by cushions rather than chairs.

The animals occupied almost all the available flat surfaces: shelves, cupboards, less accessible floor-space, even the top of the television. All were positioned with care to face the centre of the room.

Donald Duck and his nephews, bears and dogs of varying sizes, two Goofies, a hedgehog holding a spade, and many more. Some were mirrored in posters on the walls, building a house or haplessly trying to operate machinery. Easily senior amongst them was Mickey Mouse, omnipresent, staring from a dozen vantage points and even holding pride of place in the bed, in a form almost as large as Keiko herself.

Walking inside, Daniel felt himself slowed by the hot dampness of the air. He noticed that Keiko sat down stiffly, not on a cushion but close against the wall. She was still clutching her handbag and the dripping umbrella, as if she did not intend to stay long. When he sat down next to her she shifted away.

'What's up with you?' he asked. 'You've been in a filthy mood all evening.'

'Nothing wrong.' She looked away, showing him the back of her head.

'There's something – I know there is.'

She stood up, still clutching the handbag and umbrella. 'I go and make bath.'

He stood up too, taking hold of her slim shoulders with his hands. 'Don't run off. You ask me over here and then sulk and act as if I don't exist. Now what's going on?'

She twisted free and tripped away towards the bathroom. He ran after her but was too slow and reached the door as it slammed shut, just in time to hear the click of the lock sliding into place.

'Open up.'

From behind the door came the sound of the tap running.

'This is ridiculous. If something's wrong then tell me what – don't just run away.' Still no reply. 'If you don't want me round here I'll be most happy to go – most happy.' He glared at the closed door in front of him. 'All right, have it your own way.'

He marched back to the front door. The handle would not turn. He tried to shake it but it was firmly secured. He was locked in.

Back to the bathroom. 'For Christ's sake! What are you trying to do? Stop behaving like a child. Either you talk to me or you open that front door.'

Silence.

He hammered on the wood in front of him. 'This is absurd.' Striding back to the sitting-room he began searching through drawers for a key, but found none.

He had to do something, take some action. He pulled open a window, but this brought no change except to let inside a sample of the downpour. Slamming it shut he turned, plucked the hedgehog holding a spade and threw it onto the ground. A Goofy, then Donald Duck and his nephews – Daniel was punching them off shelves, throwing them down. The floor was soon littered.

Suddenly weary, he cleared a space for himself and sat

down. The sound of running water ceased and he heard the light splash of Keiko climbing into the bath.

He remembered how fond she was of all the animals. He wondered if she had heard.

Slowly he stood up and began replacing them on their shelves, trying as best as he could to remember which had been where, until the floor was clear once more.

He remembered a call he had to make to Mrs Chiba, who ran the language school where he worked. He dialled the number.

Hearing a splash from the bathroom, he imagined Keiko bursting out noisily while he was talking. He cupped his hand between his mouth and the receiver. Keiko no longer attended classes but she was still a registered student at the school. Why she continued to pay was a mystery to him. But he knew well enough the first school rule: that he, the teacher, was not allowed to see any girl students at night, except with special permission. He had no desire to have Mrs Chiba discover his involvement with Keiko.

The line clicked a connection. 'Hello, Mrs Chiba? This is Daniel. I need to speak with you about . . .'

'Danieru, yes yes,' she interrupted. 'It is lucky that you call.' She sounded excited, but then she rarely sounded otherwise. 'Big disaster is happen. Near station there is new poster advertising Happiness Institute – enemy language school.'

'I'm sorry to hear that,' began Daniel. 'But what I really rang about . . .'

'Yes yes, big disaster – they try to steal our students with this new advertisement. You must work more hard to be kind at lessons. And I have plan to build a new poster for Vital School next to enemy one – bigger poster than them.'

'Sounds great, but what I really rang to talk about was something quite different: money.'

'Danieru, Danieru,' said Mrs Chiba in a disapproving tone. 'I tell you many time before – when school is strong we can pay you all. But you must be patient.'

'I have been patient – very. And at the moment I haven't even enough to keep me alive.'

'I see. I must talk with my husband.'

Daniel stood holding the telephone, awaiting her decision. He had been working for the Chibas for some months. On the first day, before he had taught a single lesson, they had agreed a salary. Not once had he been paid anything like it. He had complained, only to be told that the school was not yet rich enough. If he remained loyal to the company he would be rewarded in the end.

After a couple of weeks of this he had begun quietly looking for other work, following advertisements in the English language daily, the *Japan Times*. But there seemed to be a glut of westerners seeking work, many of them properly qualified – unlike Daniel. He attended interviews but found nothing.

He was still writing to other schools. Mrs Chiba gave him just enough to eat and pay his rent. There were moments when he thought of threatening to sue her for all the wages he was owed. Except that he himself was breaking the law by working without a permit. And she knew it.

With a noisy click she came back on the line. 'My husband is decide,' she announced. 'He will put some money in your bank. Tomorrow it will be there.'

'How much?'

'Enough for you. Now I am busy.' She hung up.

From the bathroom came the sound of further splashing. Daniel replaced the receiver on its hook. He rearranged some of the animals – those that looked most out of place – and made his way into the cramped bedroom. He undressed, ejected the Mickey Mouse from Keiko's bed and climbed in himself.

It was not long before Keiko opened the bathroom door, releasing a cloud of steam that spread out through the sitting-room to the bedroom, making the air even hotter.

'What's up with you?' asked Daniel as she walked into the room. She gave no reply except to remove the towel draped around her, climb into the bed beside him and click off the light.

'Why ask me over if all you want to do is sulk like this?' Silence. 'Is something wrong?' He slipped his arm around her shoulders. She twisted away. 'What's going on?' he demanded. 'I've never seen you so jumpy.'

'I think you hate me,' she said quietly.

'Of course I don't hate you.'

She was not convinced. 'You never tell me things.'

'What things?'

'How long you stay in Japan.'

'But I have told you,' he said wearily. 'I don't know myself.'

She twisted beneath the sheet. 'I think you like me only for holiday girl.'

'Now wait a moment. When we first began meeting I made it quite clear that I'd only be here for a few months – you didn't seem to mind then.'

'You don't tell me about you,' she said, pronouncing the words with care. 'You don't tell me about your family.'

'I've told you, we didn't get on. And what about you? All I know about your family is that you've got one. Or the divorce. You never talk about that at all; I still don't know how it happened.'

She switched on the light and sat up, pulling the duvet up around to hide her tiny breasts. 'That is not for you.'

'It was you who started this business of knowing about each other.' He was taken aback by her reaction.

She stood up, suddenly very naked. 'I am sorry but I think you want me to go. I think I am inconvenient to you.' She picked up her handbag, as if ready to march out into the night just as she was.

'Don't be absurd,' said Daniel.

'You want me to go?'

'You can't really expect me to believe that you'll stroll out like that. And where'll you go? This is your own place.'

'You want me to go?' she repeated.

He lay back on his pillow. 'All right, all right – I don't want you to go.'

'I see.' She switched off the light and slipped back under the duvet, but lay as far from him as she could without actually falling off the bed.

He listened as her breathing slowed to a calmer tempo and tried to think back to when the affair had begun. Had he been wrong? It was not as if he had acted callously – he *had* felt strongly towards her.

In his classes at the school he had noticed her from the beginning. She had been quiet and serious, not constantly giggling like the other women. He had been impressed.

As days passed he felt more keenly his isolation in the country. He had known nobody in Japan. His one contact was a New Zealander whose address he had learnt second-hand. On arrival in Tokyo he had found the New Zealander just about to leave. He had helped Daniel find his apartment and moved on. For the first time in his life Daniel found himself spending most of each day by himself; his only regular contact with people was through his classes at Mrs Chiba's school. He came to dread Sundays, when he spent all day alone at his home.

It was on a Sunday that he met her. He had gone to buy some food from a nearby supermarket that always seemed to be open and found her staring at a shelf, pondering two brands of green tea.

He had been so relieved at the sight of a familiar face that he had greeted her as if he knew her well. She had seemed taken aback, nervous, then smiled. In the halting conversation that followed he learned that she lived only a few hundred yards from his apartment.

'Already I have seen you once,' she admitted. 'Walking on the road.'

'Why didn't you say hello?'

She gave a shy smile. 'I am too frightened to say hello to Mr Teacher.'

Only a few days later they met again, as he was walking down to the station. At a third encounter she seemed more confident and offered to take him on a tour of local shrines and temples. These were mostly modern and plain, and were barely commented on by either of them – they were far more interested in each other. Keiko mentioned how she had been divorced, and Daniel found himself intrigued by the strength of character she must possess to survive the shame of such an event in so conservative a country.

As the walk came to its end he asked her if she would like to meet for a meal. She seemed surprised, a little shocked. But she accepted.

The affair – it became an affair within just a few days – worked well enough at first. She quickly and without reserve came to show her love for him, eager to learn his every like and dislike, to pamper him. After his isolation he could have asked for nothing finer.

Their meetings began to slip into a routine. They met three or four times a week. He gave her a key to his apartment and often found her waiting there when he returned from the school, stirring some soup she had made. On Sundays they would go out for the day, to visit some temple or shrine or to see a western film, with Japanese sub-titles, in one of the central Tokyo cinemas.

She announced that she would teach him Japanese, although this never amounted to his learning more than a few words. She often joked about his ignorance of all things Japanese, calling him 'Crazy foreigner'.

'I think you are lost,' she would tell him. 'You come here by mistake. If nobody help you then I think you must die.'

There were moments, although he never voiced his thoughts to her, when he was sure they would remain together. He would take her back with him to England, or even stay on in Japan himself.

She always seemed to be there. More and more she took days off from work at a computer firm, punching cards. Her company cured him of his dread of Sundays. He began to quite enjoy time alone. And then, to his own surprise and shock, he found himself looking forward to moments of solitude.

At heart he knew even then that it was over. Or rather he half knew – most of the time he was happy enough to be with her, giving little thought to the future.

Slowly his moments of pessimism gained ascendancy. Small habits of hers began to irritate him. The way she behaved like a housewife, always cleaning his bare apartment or cooking up some soup. The way she wore schoolgirl clothes. And the animals in her apartment.

Soon the jokes about 'Crazy foreigner' were no longer at all funny, only annoying. He knew he would end the affair, but her very devotion discouraged him. He dreaded the moment. How hurt she would be. Who knew what she might do.

And he had let it go on. Till now.

Beside him her breathing was slow and regular. He wondered if he should switch on the light and have the matter out there and then. But she might be asleep. And he remembered her earlier shouting and threatening. It was not a good time; she would still be upset. Better to wait until morning. Then he would tell her that it was wrong to let matters continue, unfair to her.

She would be calmer then.

Chapter Two

The distant hum of traffic in Daniel's ears told him it was morning. He opened his eyes and saw black: thick wooden shutters excluded the light of day.

The sound that had woken him lingered: the thump of a door slamming shut. His thoughts were still hazy from sleep and it was some moments before he realized the full significance of the noise. He reached into the darkness, fingers outstretched, and found the lightswitch. Half-dazzled as he was, he could still see the empty place beside him in the bed.

He jumped up and hurried out of the room. The front door was not locked but slightly ajar. He peered out into the rain. There was no sign of Keiko; she had left for work.

With a sense of uneasiness he dressed in the centre of the living-room, watched by the many animals.

He began to walk back to his apartment. His jacket had a hood, but it was made from a thin material and he could feel the raindrops on his hair. He barely noticed the landscape around him, crowded with double-storey houses tightly crushed together, no two the same. Built from wood or concrete or corrugated iron, they all looked precariously flimsy. He thought of the events of the previous evening, annoyed at his own lack of decisiveness. He should have acted then.

His apartment was almost in sight. It was near a

shopping area and the street was lively with housewives on their way to buy provisions, carrying umbrellas and bags, wheeling or riding bicycles.

Ahead was a level crossing over the Kei Sei railway, a private line that straddled the district on its way between central Tokyo and the International Airport at Narita.

Two housewives met on the crossing and stopped to greet one another. One was weighed down with bags of shopping as well as a bicycle. As Daniel drew nearer, the air was filled with a monotone shrieking: the warning of an approaching train. Panicked by the sound, the over-burdened housewife dropped a large bag of shopping. While trying to collect it with her free hand, the bicycle toppled to the ground, then the second bag fell, spilling its groceries. She and her friend struggled to retrieve the tins and packets.

Two men in drab overalls, company workers from the nearby factory, ran to help them, plucking up the objects and ushering the women away from the line.

A small crowd quickly gathered, a hubbub of voices offering sympathy and sensible advice. The overladen housewife bowed her head in shame at having stopped in such a foolish place, repeating the word 'Sumimasen' – I am sorry. She shot a glance towards Daniel, further distressed that a foreigner should have witnessed her disgrace. The company workers smiled awkwardly, pleased but also embarrassed by their heroic role in the incident.

Daniel understood the excitement. Not long before there had been an accident on the same crossing, when a schoolgirl had caught her foot in the line. Her friend had tried to free her, but as the girl became more frightened her foot became more firmly wedged in the tracks. And then the warning siren began.

The area was scattered with level crossings and the trains passed over them at speed, soon after the barriers came down. The driver saw the two figures on the line ahead, but had no chance to brake in time. At the last moment the girl's friend managed to throw herself clear.

Daniel watched the barriers come down, slantwise, like sentries' rifles. A jumble of wheels and axles squealed past in front of him. He remembered how much the story had upset Keiko; it was she who had first told it to him. For several days she had talked incessantly of the incident: of the friend's bravery, and the grisly details of the school-girl's death.

The howling of the siren ceased and the barriers rose up. Daniel walked on towards his home. As he neared the building, he was greeted by a chorus of shouts from the windows of a school. It was break time and a number of children were leaning out towards him, triumphantly shouting '*Gaijin san, gaijin san.*' It was half-polite, meaning 'Mr Foreigner'. He knew hardly anybody in Takasago district, but he was known.

Daniel's landlord lived in a building near by. An old man, long retired, he spoke not a word of English. The rent agreement had been organized by the New Zealander, to be paid automatically from the bank account Daniel had opened. The man peered out through the window at Daniel, offering him a brief landlord's smile.

Up the stairway to his apartment. It was on the upper floor of a tiny house, so rickety that it shook gently if anything larger than a moped passed on the road below. It was built on a wooden frame designed to sway and shake and so survive earthquakes.

Daniel's part contained a bedroom and sitting-room-cum-kitchen – both hardly long enough for him to lie down – as well as a cramped bathroom. The apartment, like Keiko's, was furnished in a mixture of western and traditional styles.

The main room was western, with a thin green felt carpet on the floor. The bedroom was traditional Japanese: tatami rush matting on the floor, and no raised bed but a futon or floor mattress. Opposite, the bathroom was also traditional, the bath itself a bulky square object, tall sided so that the bather had to sit stiffly upright. It leaked.

It was not a luxurious apartment. The main room, where Daniel cooked, ate and spent most of his time, looked barely lived in. There was an minimum of furniture: steel foldable chair, low table and cushions, a child's desk that he had found dumped near by. Nor was there any decoration on the walls except a few photographs pinned above the desk. Even the windows were bare and curtainless.

The only objects arranged with care were his cameras. Placed on his desk, there were three of them, all Nikon, each with a different lens. Around them were further lenses, filters, an automatic winding device, flash and several towers of stacked film-boxes. The only possessions of value to him, he had arranged them as if they were part of a shop-window display.

As for the rest of his home, he had never felt any need to make an effort. He saw little point, as he had no idea how long he would stay in the country. He had arrived intending only to earn enough to continue travelling in Asia.

He discarded his damp jacket and sat down on the floor of the main room. Steamy though it was inside, it was still good to get out of the rain. He glanced at his watch and saw that it was barely nine. His first class at the school was not until early evening. He had time to rest before going on to Mount Takao to search for his passport.

From the low table in front of him he took a box of slides – one of many – and began feeding the contents into a viewer. One he paused to look at for some time.

It was of a family in a village in the Himalayas, basking away an afternoon on the roof of their home. The mother was clutching a baby and changing its nappies, although from the child's expression she could have been disembowelling it. An older son and daughter stood carefully watching – not because they were disgusted or curious, but because it was the main happening of that moment. Their father was trying to ignore the event, reading his book. The sun had caught his page and he was squinting. As a backdrop, behind them was the silver-blue glare of a glacier some miles away.

Daniel remembered taking the photograph. He had stood on another roof, peering through the lens for some time, waiting for their movements to coincide to form an interesting shape, and hoping that none of them would turn and see him.

Daniel's concentration on the slide was interrupted by a clang of footsteps on the stairway outside, then a light tap on the door.

For a moment he wondered if it was Keiko. But she would not bother to knock – she had her own key. Pulling open the door he discovered a short man, his face dominated by a marked squint, stiffly holding up his umbrella to shield himself from the rain. Looking down at him, Daniel felt sure he was being scrutinized, but he could not be sure as it was impossible to tell which way the man was really looking.

He pointed to a company badge on his lapel. 'I am from bank,' he explained. 'Near here bank.'

It was not the insignia of the bank Daniel used. 'It's all right. I already have a bank.'

The man shook his head. 'My bank has special offer.' He peered round Daniel into the bare apartment. 'You live here alone?' Daniel nodded and was given another question. 'How long do you stay in Japan?'

'I don't know,' said Daniel, weary at being plagued with the question again. 'Why d'you ask?'

'Question for bank – special offer.'

'But what is this special offer?'

'Soon I explain. But first please answer question. Now what is your work in Japan?'

It was at this moment that Daniel began to suspect that the man did not work for any bank. 'I have no work here,' he said carefully. 'I'm just studying Japanese.'

'At what university do you study?'

'I study alone – teach myself.' Daniel could not stop himself from glancing back into the room to see if there were any teaching-English textbooks to give him away. There were none.

'Only study?' The man surveyed him with what Daniel presumed was his good eye. 'But what for the living? A little teaching maybe?'

Daniel tried to imagine how he would behave if he were telling the truth: angry, disinterested, curious? Curious probably. He tried to fix his face into the right expression. 'No – no teaching.'

'You are sure?' The man smiled as if to encourage Daniel to take him into his confidence.

'Quite sure.'

The visitor was unwilling to give up. Again he looked round Daniel into the apartment, peering carefully at the mess of objects on the low table. He paused, perhaps hoping to be invited inside. Finally he stiffly straightened himself and bowed his head in a single, decisive nod. 'Yes. If I come here again to visit is it okay?'

'Of course.'

'Yes.' He took a step away.

'But what about the special offer?'

'No time now,' the man replied. 'Next time I will tell you.' Umbrella rigid above his head, he clattered away down the stairway.

Daniel watched him as he waddled away out of view. There was no way of being sure that he worked for the Immigration Department. It was quite possible that he did work for a bank, just as he had claimed. He could have been trying to arrange private tuition for his children. But then why the secrecy?

Either way there was nothing to be done. He had to go on teaching, despite the risk of being caught. If he were to stop, Mrs Chiba would pay him nothing at all and he would have no means of living.

Nothing to be done, no point in worrying. He picked out the possessions he needed, including one of his cameras, and put them in a canvas bag. Pulling on his jacket, still damp, he walked out into the rain.

Mount Takao was just beyond the western suburbs of Tokyo – the far side of the city from Daniel's home – and the journey was a long one. First he had to take the Kei Sei line into the city centre. He caught the last ebbs of the morning rush hour and the train was steamy and crowded.

Next he changed to the state railway that crossed the town overland. It quickly dipped into a deep moat, a defensive remnant of the Tokyo of a century before. Peering up through the window he caught sight of patches of irregular stonework. He tried to imagine what kind of city it must have been then: a medieval metropolis with foreigners firmly excluded from its walls.

The train climbed up from the moat and ahead Shinjuku became visible, the cluster of skyscrapers that marked the end of central Tokyo. Daniel changed a second time at Shinjuku station, a major junction over-crowded with passengers and platforms. He fought his way through to the one he needed.

Across the gulf of two railway tracks he watched a crowd of people waiting for a Tokyo-bound train, mutely shuffling forward to make room for others joining them. A voice shouted out in sudden outrage, the start of a high-pitched monologue directed wildly at the whole assembly. Daniel peered into the ranks, trying to pick out the owner. But he was too deeply embedded. The only visible sign of his outburst was a turning of heads.

From the far end of the platform a second shout piped up; it held the same tone of indignation. More heads turned to watch. The rainy season was beginning to take its toll.

Daniel's train drew into view. Travelling against the rush, it was not so crowded. He was able to sit down and watch the unchanging view of houses. Finally a row of hills became distinguishable through the rain. The town landscape began to break, with tiny fields showing through between the buildings. He had finally reached the far side of Tokyo. The train drew into the station for Mount Takao.

Mount Takao was a hill rather than a mountain. Not strikingly beautiful, its virtue lay in being neither too steep nor too gentle a climb, neither too high nor too low. It was proportioned exactly to the requirements of Tokyo day-trippers.

Daniel's previous visit, just a few days before, had been on the last fine weekend before the onset of the rainy season – a hazy day, air filled with the smells of green-ery and food. The three paths leading up to the summit had been teeming with people, laden down with every conceivable object from electric cookers to portable televisions. Strings of loudspeakers followed each path for its full length, issuing constant informative announcements: the names of lost children, local news, the exact air temperature and so forth.

Quite different now – the paths were empty, the loudspeakers silent. The change was very much to Daniel's liking.

He walked through the arcade of stalls and teashops at the hill's base. All were shuttered and silent – summer toys and faded boxes of camera film just visible behind burglar-proof grids. Except one solitary snack-bar. He pushed open the door.

Inside were two figures. The rain had been falling for less than a week, but on each was an expression of resigned isolation that one might have expected of lighthouse keepers. The owner stood behind the bar. The other, sitting at a table near by, wore a heavy waterproof coat over the uniform of a park official. Both showed relief when Daniel walked in, relief that their seclusion had been pierced by the unexpected appearance of a stranger, especially a foreign stranger.

Neither of them spoke more than a few words of English. Only through reference to his dictionary and by miming a search was Daniel able to explain his predicament. The official, first to understand, shook his head sadly.

'Passport is not.'

They were apologetic at being unable to help. The teashop owner insisted on preparing hot green tea and a plate of rice with sweet curry sauce. As Daniel ate, the park official picked through the dictionary, laboriously explaining that it would certainly have been found and handed in.

Daniel thanked them both, but did not return to the station. He remembered falling, somewhere on his way up to the summit, and was determined to find the spot.

The path he had taken followed the bottom of a narrow valley cut into the hill by a stream, dark semi-jungle springing out of its steep sides. At one point the land briefly opened into a clearing and the stream toppled into a waterfall that splashed into a wide pool. Next to this had been built a temple, in the centre of an enclosure of flat land. There were two low gates: one to the path and the other, oddly, leading out to the pool.

Daniel climbed higher. The valley narrowed once more, with trees closing into a canopy overhead and the stream swilling at the bottom of a small gully. It was there that he had fallen.

He searched the path, the grass verges, the edge of the vegetation, even the sopping contents of the litter bins, but without success.

Striding to and fro he noticed a point where the gully cut so close into the rock that the path ran just above it. If he had fallen there it was possible the passport had dropped down into the shallow ravine. He peered down. Although no more than ten feet deep, the sides were steep and overhanging – he could not see the bottom clearly. He might have persevered, tried to find some way down, but, half wet through as he was, he felt he had had enough.

He wondered what he would need to obtain a replacement passport. The process might involve the Japanese Immigration Department. As he neared the waterfall a sticky skein of water, cold from the icy stream, formed on his face. Looking down he saw the priest in front of his temple, lighting carefully sheltered candles. There was something in his movements, a nervous suddenness, that made Daniel curious as to what he would do next. He slowed his pace to watch.

Finished with the candles, the priest rode across the enclosure to the gate that led out to the pool. With an abrupt pull he opened it and stepped beyond. The water was shallow, no more than a few inches deep, and as he walked it tugged at his white robe.

Daniel pulled his camera from the bag and fitted a suitable lens.

The man crossed towards the waterfall until he was almost beneath it. He stood very straight, raised his hands and threw them into sudden fighting movements, karate-like blows aimed at the water hurtling down in front of him. He delayed a moment, then bowed his head into the rush.

Through the lens Daniel watched, his view interrupted by sudden blackness whenever he took a photograph. This was exactly the kind of event he was always hoping to find. His dream was to amass sufficient slides to begin selling to magazines, even to mount an exhibition. To get started.

The priest stood back from the waterfall and pulled off his robe, beneath which he was wearing a loincloth. More blows at the water – angrier now. And he stepped forward into the full force of the waterfall.

Daniel found it hard to follow his movements – the shape of his body was distinguishable only by the water ricocheting from it. He seemed to be growing smaller, collapsing under the weight of the liquid. Then Daniel realized that he had sat down. His face was just visible through the spray, mouth opening and closing; a rhythmic chanting floated across.

At least his journey had not been entirely wasted. Daniel made his way back to the station.

It was a long journey back. Zudanuma, home of the Vital International Language Institute, was far further from the centre of town even than Takasago. Outer suburb though it was, it was a bustling place. As Daniel stepped out of the station he was greeted by a roar of traffic. From one of the department stores floated down an eerie electric whine announcing four o'clock – a grotesque imitation of church bells chiming.

Zudanuma was a new town. Only a few decades before there had been little there except a railway station and a stretch of beach popular with Tokyo day-trippers. Now it was a busy centre, boasting no less than four department stores: one white, two grey and one brown-orange. They towered over the other buildings like four square cathedrals overawing a medieval city, and the gigantic cubes that were suspended above each to display the company insignia were visible for many miles.

The area even had its own red-light district, just behind Vital School.

The beach had gone, quite literally. It had been left high and dry by land reclamation projects that had pushed the sea some miles back, soon concealing it behind oil refineries and factories. It was not much mourned. After all, it would have been of little use now, with Tokyo Bay far too murky and polluted for swimming.

On a fine day, glistening behind the jagged skyline, the sea was still visible from Vital School's solitary window. the school was placed high up, in an earthquake-proof block that housed small businesses, built just outside the cluster of department stores.

Solitary window at one end, entrance at the other, it occupied what would have made one room of no outstanding size, long and narrow in shape, like a filing drawer. With plastic partitions, this area had been divided into no less than three classrooms, as well as a lavatory, a room with a sink and a reception area for Mrs Kamakura.

Mrs Kamakura was the receptionist and, Daniel suspected, resident spy for Mrs Chiba. She claimed to speak not a word of English – although she seemed to understand a great deal more than she would admit – and passed on messages to Daniel through sign language. She was quite an expert: in her youth she had been a Kabuki dancer and, despite her having since grown into the shape of a huge dormouse, the skills had not been lost.

She smiled and tilted her head to one side at Daniel as he walked into the school. He was in no mood to smile back. He had just checked his account at the bank and found he had been given a total of eight thousand yen – twenty-five pounds. His salary for a week was supposed to be more than five times as much. What he had been given was enough to survive frugally for no more than three or four days. Then he would have to go to Mrs Chiba once more.

'Chiba san,' chirped Mrs Kamakura, opening her eyes wide and pursing her lips in apology for disturbing him. Her fingers plucked up the receiver and proffered it to him. 'Chiba san,' she repeated. Deftly she tapped the number keys and a moment later he heard the familiar barking voice of Mrs Chiba.

'Danieru, Danieru – big emergency. Because of new poster of Happiness School I have decide we must find new ways to get more students – very important.'

'What new ways?'

'Many idea. Listen – after today lesson I will come to Vital with my husband and daughter and we will talk. Very important.'

'Wait a moment,' said Daniel, to prevent her from

hanging up. 'I checked my bank – there was only eight thousand in my account.'

'Danieru,' she said sadly. 'With you it is always money.'

'Only because you never give me any.'

'Later we will talk.' She rang off.

He sat down in the tiny area allotted to him, behind Mrs Kamakura's desk, and began preparing for the evening's three classes. He had to teach from a Californian textbook called *New Concept Course* which Mrs Chiba had bought cheaply. Much of it he himself had trouble understanding. As he tried to concentrate, he found his eyes wandered repeatedly to the handwritten notices that covered the walls.

One read: 'Together we all study English for good International experience at Vital International Language Institute. Now work hard now.'

They were in Mrs Chiba's unbalanced, angular handwriting, all leaning forwards and backwards at the same time.

'What is Mr Teacher saying?' asked another. 'Do you understand? No? Then you must go to Mrs Kamakura because she will help you. Yes!'

Larger than the others, one was written emphatically in capitals and even had a Japanese translation to ensure all students understood.

'YOU MUST PAY BEFORE THE END OF THE MONTH. DON'T BE LATE. DON'T FORGET.'

His student for the first lesson of the evening walked in. It was a private lesson. A sad, ugly girl shepherded through the door by her mother, also ugly but sharp-eyed and evidently determined that her daughter should triumph at English school lessons.

The girl walked ahead through the door of the classroom.

Daniel began to collect his notes and books, when the telephone rang.

Mrs Kamakura balanced the receiver in her hand, lifted it to her ear and recited in a singsong voice the full name of the school. A pause. Her face registered surprise – not the exaggeration of a theatrical reaction but genuine confusion. She repeated the school's name. A longer pause. Her eyes widened a fraction and she held out the receiver to Daniel.

First he heard sobs, then, 'I am sorry, I am sorry.' It was Keiko's voice.

Daniel held the receiver more closely to his ear, to make it more difficult for Mrs Kamakura to eavesdrop. 'I don't understand – what d'you mean?'

More sobs. 'I am sorry for what happens.'

'What happens?'

'I am bad person.' There was an audible uncertainty in her voice, as if she was still in the process of making some decision. 'You are busy and it is bad time for you. I am inconvenient.'

'It's all right.' For Mrs Kamakura's benefit he tried to sound unconcerned. 'Has something happened? What?'

A prolonged gush of sobs. Slowly she regained full control of her voice and announced, 'I am sad for the bad thing.'

'What bad thing?'

She hung up.

Daniel replaced the receiver on its hook. Uneasily aware of Mrs Kamakura watching him, he walked on to his class.

The evening's lessons did not go well. He kept remembering Keiko's call. She could have been upset from the night before. Or somebody at work might have made some unpleasant remark to her – he sometimes worried that her friends and neighbours disapproved of her involvement with a foreigner. Or had there been some other cause – he was puzzled by the way she had sounded on the edge of a decision.

His concentration was badly lacking by the time he reached the last class, an unfortunate mixture of talents that was hard to deal with.

The majority of the students were not a problem. In their early twenties, they referred to themselves as 'office ladies' and attended a whole variety of evening classes: yoga, flower arrangement, the green-tea ceremony, as well as English. Their lessons were not expected to be of practical use – their sole function was to provide evidence of a breadth of talents that was, traditionally, seen as important in making a woman fully eligible for marriage.

The office ladies wanted more to be entertained than to learn. As long as they knew enough to avoid being shamed during a class, they were content.

This was not true of two other students: Izumi and Yukio. Izumi was distinguished from the office ladies by her sense of ambition. She wanted to become a Japan Airlines hostess, for which she needed English. To Daniel, her choice of career seemed unwise. She was a sad, drooping girl behind thick glasses, with stockings that seemed to collect in despairing heaps around her ankles; and she had a natural clumsiness. Nor was she talented at languages.

Yukio was the only man in the class. His English was far from outstanding, but it was considerably more advanced than Izumi's. A minor businessman, ambitious, impatient, he had been tempted to join Vital by the low rates they charged. He resented being taught in a class with a lot of gabbling women. In particular he resented what he saw as unnecessary delays caused by Izumi's slow progress. She was well aware of his scorn. It made her all the more nervous.

Had Daniel's thoughts been less on other matters he might have remembered to begin by asking her an easy question, to put her at her ease. As it was, he asked her a hard one. She froze, then stuttered incomprehensibly until he transferred the question to one of the office ladies.

The next question he asked her was almost absurdly easy, but it came too late – her confidence was gone. She froze and stuttered while Yukio impatiently tapped a chair leg with his pencil.

Daniel would have left her in peace after that, but the last time he had done so she had complained bitterly to Mrs Chiba that he had not been teaching her properly. So he fired more questions at her. The lesson went from bad to worse, punctuated by painful pauses whenever it was her turn to answer. If she did manage to stutter a reply it would invariably be either inaudible or recognizably wrong.

Each time, Yukio expressed his irritation more clearly, scraping the legs of his chair on the floor, bursting into sudden coughing fits. Even some of the office ladies began to lose patience, hands delicately covering their mouths as they yawned.

Finally the lesson drew to an end. Daniel announced next week's work and watched as Izumi's shame transformed to anger. She packed away her books in sudden, cramped movements and hurried out ahead of the others.

As Daniel left the classroom he saw her sitting by the reception desk, excitedly voicing her dissatisfaction. Talking with her was not Mrs Kamakura, who had left, but Mrs Chiba herself. Her face made Daniel think of an angry toad, round and squat, with darting, irritable eyes. Seeing him, she motioned him to wait with an abrupt wave of her hand.

Her husband stood by the door, saying goodbye to the students as they left, smiling too much at each. A plump, soft figure, he seemed to lean backwards as he stood, while his hands floated in the air as if supporting an invisible tray. Their baby daughter crawled on the floor, mercilessly chewing something she had found.

As soon as Izumi had left, Mrs Chiba turned to Daniel, angry. 'I am very worry for her – she says she is learning nothing, that you are not kind. It is danger that she will leave – maybe join Happiness Institute.'

Daniel began to try and explain the difficulties with her and Yukio, but he was cut short.

'You must talk with her. You must tell her she is good student.'

'But she's the worst in the school.'

'I think you must sit down and drink coffee with her – in the classroom after lesson,' barked Mrs Chiba. 'Tell her she is good student with coffee and she will believe. You will?'

'You want me to lie?'

She gave him a disapproving glare. 'You must be good teacher for school.' She stood up, waving to her husband to collect the daughter. 'I wanted to talk of new ways to find students but now I am too busy.' Her tone was touchy and hurt, implying that it was his, Daniel's, fault. 'Even I had wanted to go for a meal in restaurant – all of us and I pay. Impossible. Even still now I will take you to the station.'

Daniel was not taken in by the cancelled offer of a meal – she had never been known to buy anybody anything before. Quite the opposite. She had become very vocal on an occasion when Daniel had accidentally pocketed a pencil from Mrs Kamakura's desk.

More surprising than the offer of dinner was that she had not raised the matter of Keiko's phone call. Perhaps Mrs Kamakura had not told her. It did not seem very likely.

They filed out. Usually when the Chibas visited the school they gave him a lift back to a station near their home; it was on the Kei Sei line and so made his journey easier, saving him a change.

As they walked out of the building he watched her ankles at work on the rain-sodden pavement ahead of him. Tightly packed, they clipped briskly on the flag-stones, stamping to a halt beside the car.

'Bad place,' she announced as she opened the driver's door. The car was parked in a narrow street behind the school, amongst the flickering signs of the red-light district. At the end rose up the flat, incongruous façade of a medieval castle, Disney style. It was the frontage of a love hotel, where rooms could be rented out by whores and their clients or by couples seeking to evade the scrutiny of their families.

'Bad place,' repeated Mrs Chiba as she switched on the engine.

She weaved dangerously into the traffic, red rearlights in the rain. In the back her husband struggled to control the daughter, who was wailing when they reached the house and her father carried her out, warily, as if she were hot to touch.

Mrs Chiba drove on, silent until they reached the station. Daniel opened the car door but she took hold of his sleeve.

'One moment. Now, isn't there something you want to tell me?'

'I don't understand.'

Mrs Chiba sighed crossly. 'I hear young girl calls you at the school today.'

'Yes, a friend of mine. So what?'

'I hear she is cry very much.'

'Maybe she did. What business is it of yours?'

Mrs Chiba shook her head. 'School business. You know that teacher must not take girl student back to his house or even go out with her at night. I have told you many times. Now – do you have something to tell me?'

'I'm afraid not.'

She gave out a dissatisfied snort. 'Very bad,' she said in a warning voice. 'Very bad that you make secret from your employer.'

Daniel opened the door. 'It's none too good if the employer spends all her time spying on her teacher.'

'Maybe she must.'

There was a pause in the rain as Daniel walked back to his apartment. From the half-covered sewer that ran alongside the road rose up clouds of evil-smelling steam. Ahead he saw light shining out from his curtainless windows. Keiko was there.

Pushing open the door, he could feel the oppressive steaminess inside. Keiko had been cooking – a savoury smell hung in the air. Hearing him come in she tripped across the room, all Mickey Mouse socks and brightly coloured teenage clothes. She halted him with an embrace, lightly clinging. He unclasped her.

'What's been going on? Why did you call me at the school?'

She reached up and covered his mouth with a finger. 'Later we talk – first we eat. You are sleepy.' She turned back to the cooker.

'I'm not sleepy or hungry. I just want to know why you rang me.'

She stirred the soup she had made. It was thin and dark, full of anonymous ingredients. 'Good food – for healthy man.'

He was beginning to lose patience. 'I know there was a reason. You said there was something that was happening.'

'Hungry hungry makes angry,' she chirped. 'Angry angry.'

He slammed his fist down on the sideboard, making the pan jump with a clang on its gas ring. Keiko looked up, confused and scared by the violence of his action. At once he felt ashamed.

'I'm sorry. I didn't mean to frighten you. But I do want to know why you rang me at the school.'

'Yes.' She spoke very quietly. 'I was at work. I remember bad things I say yesterday. Suddenly I am fright you will hate me, that you will say goodbye. So I call. After then I know I am wrong – I come back to make soup, for sorry.'

He was not sure whether to believe her or not. He felt sickened – with her, with himself.

'You are still angry?' she asked.

'No, not angry.' He tried to summon strength. 'I think we'd better talk.'

'Yes, talk,' she said thoughtfully. She glanced down at the pan on the cooker. 'But before talk there is soup.'

'No, let's get this settled now.'

She threw a glance to him, filled with mock anger. 'Why? You hate my soup?'

'I didn't say that.'

'You only like foreign soup?'

He had no intention of being sidetracked. 'Look – I don't want to talk about that.'

'So you do hate my soup,' she said haughtily. She stood up. 'I am angry.'

'Keiko . . .'

She turned on her heels and tripped away towards the bathroom. With a nasty sensation of *déjà vu*, Daniel jumped after her. Too late. The door slammed shut and was locked before he reached it. He hammered on the frosted glass. 'Will you come out of there?'

'I do not speak to man who is so rude.' She turned on the tap.

'This is a serious matter.'

She began singing.

He decided to wait until she emerged – she could not lock herself away for ever.

He returned to the sitting-room; but hardly had he opened a book to read when he heard the click of the latch sliding back. The door remained closed. Quietly he made his way back to the bathroom. He threw open the door.

The air was heavy with steam but still he saw her clearly. She was sitting on the edge of the bath, facing him. She wore a thin cotton kimono that she used as a bath-robe. It was not tied and fell loosely around her, covering little more than her shoulders. Previous intentions began to slip from his mind – he had forgotten how attractive she could be.

'Why do you come here?' she asked, with mock alarm.

'To talk,' he said mechanically.

She glanced pertly at him. 'Only talk?'

'No – I mean . . .' He had lost the thread.

'Foreign man is so rude.' She shook her head dis-approvingly and slid down from the bath towards him. Her expression was stern, as if giving an admonishment. She reached out, took his hand and drew it beneath her kimono to the soft skin of her waist.

'So rude.'

He knew what he had planned to do – what he should do. But he did not. Instead he leant down and kissed her.

Much later they lay side by side in the darkness, both still silky with the heat of what had gone before. Except for the light tapping of rain on the roof, the air was quite silent. Daniel's breathing was slow and regular, his thoughts in the midst of blurring into unconsciousness when he heard Keiko's voice murmur, 'What do you do tomorrow day?'

'Nothing,' he replied, just awake enough to be faintly puzzled by the question.

Chapter Three

Daniel's eyes opened narrowly and blinked at the strong light. In through the window shone the sun, the sky behind it an untarnished blue – a gap in the rainy season. The glass seemed to magnify the heat; the tiny room was uncomfortably hot. Daniel struggled against a sense of lassitude and sat up.

Keiko lay beside him, entangled in the sheet. He glanced at his watch and saw that it was after ten. He nudged her. She should have already been at work.

'It's late. Aren't you going to your job?'

She did not move, murmuring reluctantly, 'Too tired.'

'Aren't you even going to ring them?'

'Not want.'

The events of the previous night began to trickle back to him. Breathing in the hot air, he felt a sudden need to get away from the apartment, from Keiko, if only for a few minutes. He climbed up from the bed to wash and dress.

Outside the front door the air was reassuringly fresh, almost cool after the stuffiness of the apartment. He stood for a moment, enjoying the sensation of release. He saw his bicycle, secured just below, and decided to go for a ride, enjoy the fine weather while it lasted.

The bicycle was second-hand, if not more, and showed its age in flaking paintwork, a dented and twisted frame, and disfigured saddle. But it had been strongly built and on it Daniel had explored much of the neighbourhood.

This was no small achievement. The way the local streets curved and turned, it was as if they had been deliberately designed to confuse. The area was residential, a maze of small houses cracked by the constant minor earthquakes. For landmarks there were only a river, the local private railway, a water tower, and the insignia cube of a distant department store. On his journeys Daniel almost invariably became lost. He hoped he might stumble across some temple or garden previously concealed within the folds of the district. He very rarely did.

A wind was blowing in strong gusts. Aware that the weather might change quickly, he decided not to risk losing his way, choosing to cycle alongside the river to the nearby park.

The sun was making progress in drying out the sodden air; steam was rising copiously from the half-covered sewers and more persistent puddles. He soon reached the river bank. The path sat astride the flood wall and gave a fine view down over Takasago, a carpet of ragged houses with the occasional interruption of a box-shaped mesh of green netting – a baseball practice centre – or the rickety chimney of a communal bath. In the distance across the river was the taller skyline of central Tokyo.

Daniel's destination was no traditional garden, filled with symbolic waterfalls, ponds, and paths. Like most Japanese parks its purpose was purely practical: to provide space on public holidays for the greatest possible number of picnicking Japanese.

Almost bare of trees or any vegetation, it was empty and bleak. But behind it lay an oxbow lake of the river that had somehow survived destruction for the creation of more houses. Along its bank Daniel found three anglers, old men wearing baseball caps to protect themselves from the sun. Deep in concentration, they did not seem to notice his arrival. He laid his bike down on the ground and sat on the damp grass.

Staring up at the blue sky, enjoying the dry warmth of the sun, his thoughts began to wander. It was hard now to understand how he had become so worried. After all, had anything actually occurred?

He was woken by a light splash. Sitting up he watched the nearest of the three fishermen haul out of the water a large grey fish. It twitched half-heartedly. With a stick the fisherman struck its head – short, quick blows – until it was still. As he turned to drop it into his sack, he saw Daniel and flinched, eyes quickly looking away, surprised by the sight of a foreigner, embarrassed by his surprise.

Daniel lay back in the grass. But he was unable to regain the feeling of drowsiness. He could not make himself comfortable, was bothered by the dampness, by the parade of ugly houses beyond the water, by the presence of the fishermen. He stood up and raised his bicycle from the grass.

He decided not to take the same route back – the sky was clear and he felt he could afford to risk a slow return. In a short time he had lost himself in the maze of buildings. From amongst them came the rasping of machinery, small family workshops turning out parts for the production lines of large corporations – uneconomic in size, surviving by sheer long hours.

The wind began gusting more keenly than before, slowing Daniel's progress and filling the sky with ragged clouds. Rain would quickly follow. Between the houses Daniel glimpsed the insignia cube of a familiar department store and realized that he was travelling in quite the wrong direction. He turned about.

The first rain began to fall, oversized leaden drops

indicating a coming downpour. He tried to keep track of the slight but repeated twists in the roads, only to glimpse again the department store insignia – once more he had edged off course into a full U-turn.

The downpour began. The road became a shallow stream, dancing with watery detonations. Daniel stopped and pulled up the hood of his jacket, but the rain was soon streaming down his face. Already quite drenched, he reached a line of the Kei Sei railway. Which part it was or from which direction he was approaching he had no idea. He pressed on, in the hope of finding a landmark to help him or a coffee shop where he could shelter.

Finally the rain began to relent. Weaving through the twisting roads his eye was caught by a large black car, parked on a corner, its windows darkened. He had never seen anything so huge in the district. As he passed, he glanced inside. It was empty.

Looking up, he was surprised to see that it was the corner of his own street. His apartment was just a few yards away.

His shoes squelched uncomfortably as he made his way up the stairway. Inside, he crouched in the alcove for removing footwear – in his case, particularly urgent. The laces were swollen and hard to pick free. When he had finally succeeded and looked up it was to see, standing in the centre of his room, a man he had never before set eyes on.

His hair was beginning to grey but there was no frailty about him. Stocky for a Japanese, his most striking feature was his eyes, unmoving and direct. Daniel felt as if they were staring through him. There was a charged stillness to his whole being, like a top spinning at great speed that appears motionless.

He did not look like a burglar. He seemed so at ease that

it might have been his flat and Daniel could have been the intruder.

For a moment they stood staring at one another. Then Daniel called out, 'Who are you?'

The man gave him a glare, as if the question were prying. 'Harada, of course.'

Daniel did not like the sound of this statement. The 'Of course' seemed particularly inauspicious.

Keiko was at the cooker, head bowed as she chopped vegetables, visibly keeping out of the meeting.

Recovering from his surprise, Daniel proffered a hand to the visitor. The man hesitated before shaking it, as if considering whether it might be diseased.

An awkward pause. Daniel expected the man to give an explanation for his unexpected presence. After all, he had not been invited. But Mr Harada seemed to be unaware of any such need. He glanced disparagingly around the bare room.

'What brings you here?' asked Daniel at last.

The guest directed towards him another glare of disapproval. 'Visit of course.'

'But what kind of visit?'

Mr Harada pondered for a moment. 'I think friendly.'

Daniel crossed to Keiko at the cooker. 'Your father – is he staying for lunch?'

She nodded quickly.

'Is something wrong?'

'I am so sorry – so many things to do.' She picked up some vegetables and put them in a pan, turning her back to him.

Daniel was not enjoying the sensation of feeling unwelcome in his own apartment. He went to the bedroom to change out of his rain-soaked clothes.

Once out of the stifling atmosphere of the sitting-room

he found it easier to think. He remembered Keiko's question late the previous night: 'Do you go out to-morrow day?' She must have known even then that her father would pay a visit – that was why she had not gone to work. It had been planned.

The sooner he discovered what was going on the better. Pulling on a dry shirt, he determined to try to begin a conversation, deflate the awkwardness that had developed. He walked through to Mr Harada.

'I'm glad you could come – I've wanted to meet some of Keiko's family. Have you come far?'

The man stared at him, a warning blankness in his eyes, as if puzzled by Daniel's persistent rudeness. 'Why do you ask?'

'I was just curious.'

'Not so far,' he said, admitting to the fact with reluctance.

Daniel was baffled by the man's stonewalling. Was it from anger at his involvement with his daughter? Or did he simply not like foreigners? For a moment he toyed with the idea of loudly demanding an explanation. But it might be unwise. Better to wait until he knew more.

It promised to be quite a wait. Mr Harada betrayed no concern at the tense quiet. His face showed disinterest, as if the whole gathering could not have been more natural. His mouth remained firmly closed even when the soup was ready on the table and the three of them sat down to eat. For an instant the silence was broken: the father and daughter chanted *Ita dekimasu*, the Japanese equivalent of grace. Then nothing.

Daniel watched the two of them eating: Keiko quickly, head bowed, looking down into her bowl; her father unhurried, catching each piece of food with care. Perhaps he had really just come for a visit and no more, out of curiosity to meet Daniel. It did not seem very likely.

Mr Harada finished eating well after his daughter or Daniel. Plucking a last piece of food from his bowl he chewed thoughtfully and swallowed. Replacing his chopsticks on the table he pushed away the empty bowl. With a grunt he told his daughter to make tea. She stood up at once to obey. His expression a shade mellower, he turned to Daniel.

'I do not hate you – you must understand.'

'But I don't understand,' said Daniel. 'Why should you hate me?'

'Many foreigner are bad,' said Mr Harada thoughtfully, quite ignoring the question. 'Some are hippy foreigner – many drug, many women. Very bad. In Japan we hate hippy very much. But you are not like hippy. I do not hate you, even for what you have done.'

'What d'you mean? What are you saying I've done?'

Mr Harada gave him a disapproving glare for the interruption. 'You are not bad man. I know you will be kind to my daughter and her child.'

'What child?'

Mr Harada screwed up his eyes, puzzled by his ignorance or stupidity . 'My daughter's child – your child.'

'But there isn't one.'

'Not now,' said Mr Harada patiently, 'but soon.'

'You mean . . .'

Mr Harada nodded, as if the question had been voiced. Daniel stood up, stumbled across to Keiko, still fidgeting by the kettle. 'Is this true?'

'True,' she said quietly.

'But it can't be.' Even as he spoke the words he began to lose faith in them. There had been that time, the first time, in this same room – hurried and impatient, an ungainly scrabble of bodies and clothes. There had been no thought of precautions.

'Why didn't you tell me?' he asked.

'I was frighten.'

'It's not a problem,' said her father. 'My daughter is lucky to find good westerner who will look after her.'

'But you don't understand,' spluttered Daniel. 'I'm not going to live here. I'm only staying in Japan a few months and then I'm going travelling.'

Mr Harada seemed not to have heard a word that he had said. 'Now I have told you news,' he announced, taking a step back towards the door. 'You must meet all my family – they will like you I think.'

'But you don't . . .'

'It is good that you come for tomorrow lunch, if you are convenient.'

'It's not the time, it's . . .'

'Of course my house is not easy to find – I will send my car. It will arrive at twelve-thirty.'

'But it's impossible.'

Mr Harada slowly turned to face him, all mellowness gone. 'You refuse to meet my family.'

'No . . . I mean . . .'

He nodded, reluctantly satisfied. 'Good. Tomorrow.'

'But . . .' Daniel could think of no proper reply. He watched as Mr Harada marched down the stairway, Keiko just behind him, and they crossed the road to the car. It was the one he had noticed earlier – unusually large, black, with darkened windows.

The rain was still falling but Daniel hardly noticed. Walking in it was far preferable to sitting in the apartment.

He knew what Mr Harada expected of him. Without actually stating it the man had made his demand very clear.

Daniel imagined how it would be. Keiko would stay at home; the perfect wife, supportive of her husband, looking after the children.

Whether in Japan or England he would find himself teaching – he would need to find work quickly or he would be unable to support his family. He would hate it. Occasionally he would give vent to an explosion of resentment towards his wife, for sealing him into such an existence. Each time she would be confused and frightened. Afterwards he would hate himself for having behaved as he had.

He reached his destination, one of the few places in the neighbourhood where it was possible to sit down.

Several hundred years old, it was one of the best known shrines in Tokyo, largely because of a long running series of comedy films that had been shot in the area. Like Mount Takao it was popular with the day-trippers and, on fine weekends, was crowded with people. But on this, a rainy weekday, Daniel had the place to himself.

He sat on the top step of the main building; behind him an incense-heavy hall, busy with the paraphernalia of Shintoism: cohorts of statues of varying sizes and colours, bowls piled with food offerings: rice, oranges, even an opened can of sweetened coffee from a drinks machine. In the courtyard in front of him were larger objects, including a heavy metal chest into which coins were thrown for prayers, and a covered ornamental brazier, from out of which issued a thin stream of smoke.

He looked up at the eaves above him and watched thick beads of water slide fitfully along the underside of the guttering. At the very edge they quivered with their own weight, until it was so great that they fell and shattered on the paving with a dull tap.

He had no inkling how common abortions were in

Japan, a conservative country. But as he pondered the idea he decided that it could be significant that Mr Harada had not actually mentioned the word marriage. He might be open to alternatives.

Daniel knew he would have to show he was aware of the seriousness of the matter, that he was sorry for what had happened, nor irresponsible like a 'hippy'. He could think of only one way of proving this: by paying for the operation. He could do so if Mrs Chiba paid all the money he was owed.

He peered out across the courtyard. Beyond the shelter of the shrine roof the veil of rain had thinned to a misty drizzle. The dull taps of drops falling from the guttering became slower. Then their patter became confused with another, similar sound. Daniel looked up at the wooden gateway and saw Samuel Echtbein, his three Japanese sons in a row behind him, each beneath his own umbrella, tallest at the front, shortest at the back.

'Whad'ya know – just the man I was looking for,' Echtbein called out, raising his stick in greeting. 'I've just been knocking at your front door – wanted a chat.'

Daniel felt in no mood for company, least of all for a 'chat'. He watched as Echtbein gave each of his sons a coin. Tallest first, they threw them into the chest, clapped their hands to wake the gods, pressed their palms together, and bowed their heads in prayer.

'How're you doing?' asked Echtbein, sitting down beside Daniel on the steps.

'Surviving,' he replied, unconcealed reluctance in his voice.

'Glad to hear it.' Echtbein was undiscouraged. 'I thought you looked a little down when I ran into you the other evening.'

'I was fine.'

Echtbein nodded. 'Nice looking girl you were with.' Scratching his chin he watched his sons as they strode around the edge of the courtyard, inspecting the confusion of the artefacts scattered across it. 'In fact that's what I wanted to chat with you about.'

'It's not a good time – I've rather a lot to think about at the moment.'

Echtbein's face shifted minutely into a faint smile. 'Surely you can spare five minutes to listen to a guy who knows this country a little better than you.'

There was no escaping him.

'Not that I don't get a little confused myself,' he went on. 'In fact . . .' He allowed himself another ghost of a smile. 'In fact sometimes I think the longer you stay here the less you understand. But what I really want to say is that you gotta remember that people do things differently over here.'

'Is that so?'

Echtbein's brow was clouded by a flicker of a frown. 'Now I don't want to sound like an old school ma'am – I don't even know what your situation is – but I feel I ought to tell you that you're in a very old-fashioned country. I mean if a guy asks a girl out over here it means a good deal more than it would back in the States or England. And if he takes her back to his place, well, she may take that as saying quite a lot.'

Daniel glanced at his head – the thick glasses and closely cropped, dome-shaped skull gave him an insect-like appearance. 'And what if she's divorced?'

'Divorced? That's kinda unusual over here.' Echtbein scratched his chin again, taking in the new information. 'It's sorta taboo in Japan – very hard for a divorced woman to remarry. Of course, if she met a westerner she might hope that he wouldn't mind that she'd already been married once – it's well known that divorce isn't so much of a business in the West.'

'I see.'

'I feel that I have a kind of duty to make sure that foreigners over here behave themselves – that they don't start giving a bad impression.'

Daniel glared at the three sons, now examining the brazier-like object. 'I think I can imagine all right.'

Echtbein nodded. 'I might just drop in sometime anyway – make sure you're okay.'

'There's no need.' The sharpness in his voice caused the three sons to look round at him.

'It's no trouble.' Echtbein planted the rubber end of his stick on the ground and raised himself up, waving to his sons that it was time to go.

'I can look after myself.'

'I think I might just drop in anyway,' said Echtbein slowly.

'You don't even know the girl.'

'Then perhaps it's time I did.'

On his way back to the apartment Daniel paused to stare into the window of a television shop. On ten screens the same couple walked through idyllic countryside – an advertisement of some kind, presumably aimed at newly-weds. The boy looked hardly more than sixteen, although his expression was serious and responsible. The girl seemed even younger, skipping through the grass by his side. The clothes she wore were like Keiko's.

Chapter Four

'What will you do this weekend?' An innocent enough question, or so it seemed to Daniel.

Noriko, the housewife he had asked, could barely conceal her pleasure in replying. 'I will play tennis with my husband.' She paused for maximum effect. 'At private tennis school we are join.'

'Good. At *the* private tennis school we *have* joined,' corrected Daniel. After making Noriko repeat the answer he turned to put the question to Kyoko, the second housewife. Unable to offer anything so prestigious as a private tennis school, she bowed her head and stammered, 'I will go shopping and cook meals for my husband.'

'Good. And you, Chizuru – what will you do?'

Chizuru was the youngest and most fashionable of the housewives – her hairstyle was faintly punk. She nodded cheerfully at the question. 'I will go with my husband to play of new Japanese writer Takehashi Kuniyo: *The Water Pool of Police*. I know actor in this.'

Listening to Daniel correcting Chizuru's plan, Kyoko became all the more crestfallen. Noriko was unperturbed. She smiled gratefully. 'I know this play,' she volunteered. 'Two nights ago I have seen it.'

'Did you like it?' asked Daniel.

'I do not hate it so much,' she admitted, tilting her head slightly. 'It's a little interesting, although my husband says it is long and traditional. I hope Chizuru will enjoy it.'

Attacking the play as too old-fashioned had its effects. Chizuru glanced down at her copy of the textbook, as if growing bored by the whole discussion.

The housewives attended classes for quite different reasons from the office ladies. They had found their husbands and so had no need to impress, except as a form of one-upmanship. Instead they joined the school to break up an otherwise monotonous day in their homes. It was a social event. Afterwards the three of them would go to one of the family restaurants at the top of a nearby department store and share a gossipy lunch.

To Daniel it was a minefield. He had to try and keep the sniping comments under control. If one of them was shamed too badly she would leave the class. He also had to work hard at remaining impartial. If he appeared to favour any housewife over the others this would certainly be remarked upon to his employers.

On that particular day, too, the class was awkwardly timed. It left him little more than an hour to return to his apartment and ready himself for the meeting with Keiko's family.

'Any questions?' he asked, bringing the lesson to an end. There were none. Chizuru plucked up her raincoat – it was new and fashionably cut. She slipped it on with a slight flourish, as if to show her lack of interest in other people's opinions of plays. Noriko put on her own drab raincoat, seeming not to notice the gesture.

Daniel opened the classroom door and heard the telephone ringing. He went to answer it – Mrs Kamakura took her place only in the evening – and heard a familiar barking voice.

'Hello, Danieru, hello?'

'Hello Mrs Chiba – I've been trying to get through to you for ages . . .'

'Yes yes – I am busy. And now I have new student for you.'

'What I have to say – it's important.'

'Important I know,' she interrupted. She was a practised hand at preventing others from speaking: she spoke so quickly and noisily that it was like trying to talk down railway announcements. Daniel resigned himself to hearing her out.

'Important private student for you. Businessman. He wants to go to America soon and needs lesson immediately. He will come back to the school in one hour to meet you.'

'But I won't be here.'

Mrs Chiba released an indignant cough-like sound. 'But you must – for school.'

'I can't – I'm having lunch with some . . . some friends.'

'What friend?' she demanded.

'Just some friends.'

'Japanese?'

'Yes, Japanese.'

'I see,' she said stiffly. 'More secrets, yes? Well, I call another time, maybe.'

'But there's something else I have to talk with you about – something important. You see there's a problem with money . . .'

'Already we talk.'

'But this is different . . .'

'No – I am so busy.' She hung up.

Daniel rang back but the line was engaged – she had taken the phone off the hook.

A hurried journey back to the apartment. He arrived only a few minutes before the Haradas' car was due. He was still shaving – he had woken late and had no chance to do so before the housewife class – when he heard the clang of footsteps on the stairway. He quickly wiped the foam from beneath his ears and slung on a jacket; he did not bother with a tie.

Opening the door he found not Mr Harada but a man no older than himself, dark glasses over his eyes, one hand holding a cigarette while the other was raised in greeting.

'Hi. I am Toshihiko – Keiko's brother.'

The car with darkened windows was parked below. Climbing into the driver's seat, Toshihiko switched on a cassette.

'American music,' he announced approvingly. 'You know America?'

'No, only England.'

'England,' he repeated, a touch scornfully. 'But I think America is better.'

'Bigger.'

Toshihiko nodded. 'Better.' He shook his head in time to the music as he drove, past the ramshackle houses, trickling sewers and out over a grey river, towards the north-east. His tastes may have been western but his every movement was abrupt and Japanese.

As they passed further from Takasago, the houses grew larger, their walls less cracked, while some even had small gardens. Finally they reached an area of narrow winding roads. They parked in front of a house large enough to dwarf three of the one that contained Daniel's apartment.

Toshihiko slipped his dark glasses into a jacket pocket before leaving the car. His father emerged to meet them while they were still in the entrance alcove, standing over Daniel as he struggled to remove his shoes.

'Welcome to my family.'

As his son trotted away, he led Daniel through to a

dining-room, palatially spacious for Tokyo, walls painted a garish scarlet, and at the far end a long table topped with green-tinged glass.

Daniel barely noticed the décor. He was more concerned with the knot of relatives standing nearer to hand. All were men, all wearing a jacket and tie – except, of course, Daniel himself. The sheer number of them seemed to indicate that it was a meeting between Daniel and his prospective in-laws, hardly the ideal opportunity to talk of abortions and money. He would have to try and speak to Mr Harada after the meal.

Daniel was introduced to Masayuki, Toshihiko's older brother, an individual so gorilla-shaped that Daniel found it hard to believe that he was really related to the others. The only clear point of resemblance to his father was in the eyes. Both possessed the same look of shuttered stillness.

The other relatives were more remote: two uncles with streamlined faces and narrow eyes, a number of anonymous cousins and nephews, and a Mr Toshio, who had thick mask-like skin and was introduced not as a family member but as connected with Mr Harada's company.

Mrs Harada, small and weary, was busy shuttling bowls of food to the table, as was an even tinier grandmother, and Keiko herself. Daniel was surprised to see that she was no longer wearing brightly coloured teenage clothes. She had changed to more sober Japanese housewife-wear.

He found himself being addressed by Masayuki, the older brother, who seemed to have almost no English.

'Liquorish people like fit,' he announced.

'Liquorish?'

'Big fit – Falklando fit.'

'What fit?'

'Liquorish and Arkintina.'

'You mean the Falklands fight.'

Masayuki nodded and raised a huge clenched fist, grinning with approval. 'Liquorish strong.' He un-clenched the fist. 'Japan people like Kendo, Sumo, Karate – what fit you Liquorish like?'

'Cricket?'

Masayuki looked puzzled. 'Dangeriz?'

'Very.'

The meal was ready. Daniel was seated between Mr Harada, at the end of the table, and mask-faced Mr Toshio, with Keiko opposite, silently staring down into the bowl in front of her, seemingly subdued by the whole occasion.

The food was consumed largely in silence. Daniel imagined this was because few of those present could manage English – it would be poor manners to speak in Japanese and to leave him, the guest, in the dark.

There was beer on the table and occasionally Mr Harada would punctuate the quiet with a toast.

'Good meeting of nation people. *Campai.*'

'Families of Harada and Danieru. *Campai.*'

'Happy life for Danieru in Japan. *Campai.*'

As the meal drew towards its end, Mr Toshio turned to Daniel. 'You are English teacher?' he asked. When Daniel said he was the man nodded thoughtfully. 'Interesting. In Mr Harada's company many people like English.'

'Do they?'

'Yes. You like your now teaching school?'

'Very much. Very much indeed.'

'Interesting.' He nodded thoughtfully again.

The meal was over. Guests stood up and began to trail towards the door. Daniel summoned courage and made his way through to Mr Harada.

'I'd like to talk to you.'

Mr Harada glanced past him, polite but uninterested. 'Yes – me also.'

'I don't think you understand – a talk in private.'

'Private talk – yes, it is good idea. Soon maybe.'

'No – I mean now.'

'Yes – a talk,' said Mr Harada more sternly, signalling to Toshihiko. 'Now my son will drive you back to your house.'

'But I need to speak with you.'

'Yes, I think so.' He turned away.

Toshihiko put on his shades as soon as he was in the car and hummed American music throughout the journey back. Daniel glared out of the landscape beyond the darkened windows, until they pulled up below his apartment. As he climbed out of the car, Toshihiko gave an abrupt wave.

'G'bye. See ya next week.'

'Why? What's happening next week?'

Toshihiko shrugged his shoulders, suddenly aware that he had said too much. 'See you maybe.'

The last lesson of the evening was Keiko's old class. Daniel followed his students out of the classroom: two giggling schoolgirls and Sugio, a grey-haired office worker with faint stubble on his chin, as well as a gaggle of office ladies, joking and tittering at mistakes they had made during the lesson. As he watched them file out, Daniel wondered what they would think if they knew about him and Keiko.

He stopped at Mrs Kamakura's desk to ask her to call Mrs Chiba for him. She lightly tapped the keys of the telephone, listened, then tilted her head apologetically, holding the receiver up so he could hear the hollow ringing sound. No reply.

He stamped his feet as he made his way down the

stairway and out into the rain, glaring at the commuters hurrying past. Why was it impossible to talk directly with anyone? Either they were too busy, or out, or prickly about being questioned, or just downright evasive.

The electric whine droned down from one of the department stores, announcing ten o'clock. He thought of the chiming of bells it was trying to resemble. June in England. The best month. No rainy season there. He imagined clear skies over open, lush countryside. Long evenings.

A shout of warning from behind and he fell sprawling to the ground. An office worker had slipped in the wet and cannoned into him. The man was already scrambling to his feet, nervously chanting apologies.

'For Christ's sake.' Daniel heard his own voice shouting out, strangely loud.

The office worker apologized all the more urgently.

'Why can't you just make yourselves clear, say what you mean?'

Passers-by cast brief, anxious glances towards the foreigner sitting on the wet pavement, bawling up at them. The office worker stepped backwards. '*Sumimasen.*' He bowed and scurried away.

As Daniel pulled himself to his feet, he heard a chuckle behind him.

'Something get you down mate?' The accent matched the shapeless baggy clothes, the uniform of travelling Australians. 'You look as if you're ready to jump off Tokyo Tower with the next bunch of suicide cases.'

'A few things have been getting on my nerves, that's all,' said Daniel.

'Not surprised in this shithouse country.' The Australian scratched his beard, a goatee which he seemed proud of, as if he believed it made him look artistic. 'You're a

Brit aren't you. You know you're the first roundeye I've met in this whole district. And I've been teaching here almost a month.'

'Where?'

'Happiness Language Institute it's called – cranky place in some sheds by the motorway.'

Daniel explained that he worked at Vital.

'Wondered who was up there,' said the Australian. 'I even paid the place a visit once, but when I said where I worked the old bat in charge shooed me out like I had the pox.'

'That must've been Mrs Chiba.'

'Yeah, that was the name. Listen Brit, whad'ya say we go and have a drink and compare notes on this bastard country, eh? Us foreigners gotta stick together.'

Daniel paused. He did not trust the Australian. He was too glib, his eyes were too narrow. But it was so long since he had had a fluent conversation in his own language. He had a thirst to speak without picking words that would be easily understood. And he needed to tell somebody about the Haradas – anybody.

'All right – let's have a drink or two.'

They went to a Japanese pub, a subterranean den, its walls covered with wooden slats displaying prices in painted characters. The benches were well packed with students from the nearby technical college, celebrating a Saturday night.

Daniel found the sight of the beer in front of him comforting. He drank quickly, as did Jake, the Australian. Before long they were each on their third bottle and Daniel had recounted the events of the previous few days.

'Just tell 'em to shove off,' advised the Australian.

'I don't think that'd be a good idea.'

'What else are you going to do? You said yourself you don't want to get hitched to the daughter.'

'It's not that simple.'

The Australian shook his head. 'See it this way mate. You don't want to marry her, right? Well, they're not gonna love you, whatever you do. So there's no point in larking about offering them money. Tell 'em to scram and save yourself the bother.'

'I can't treat them like that.'

' 'Course you can. The trouble with you poms is you're all so bleeding wet. They haven't a leg to stand on. You haven't promised her anything. You're not even living together.'

'But I got her pregnant.'

'Probably brought it upon herself deliberately. Half the girls in Nippon want to get themselves married off to one of us *gaijin* – God knows why. Just tell her you're not falling for it.'

'It's not so easy. You haven't met these people – there's something about them.'

There was a commotion at the bar. The staff were shouting an announcement, the students clamouring for more drinks.

'Looks like they're closing.' Daniel swallowed the last of his beer.

'Doesn't matter,' announced Jake. 'I know a good few places that stay open late.'

'I ought to be getting back.'

'But we've hardly started. Are you really in such a rush to get back to all that misery with your girlfriend's folks?'

He had a point. Daniel glanced at his watch and saw that the last train did not leave for almost three-quarters of an hour. If he missed it he could probably sleep on the floor at Jake's place. He must live nearby.

'All right – one more drink.'

'That's the way Brit. I know a great place round here – place with a bit of character.'

They made their way out into the warm rain, past the station and department stores, to the area of narrow streets just behind Vital School. The rain-filled air was lit by flickering lights, and signs with amateurish photographs of women baring their bodies.

The bars were closing, their owners turning down lights to try to entice their customers to leave. Clusters of office workers staggered to and fro, ties askew. Daniel saw one clutching a lamppost, retching, a colleague standing patiently near by, holding both their umbrellas.

The façade of the love hotel loomed towards them. Out of the entrance stepped an office worker with a small dark-skinned girl.

'She doesn't look Japanese,' observed Daniel.

'She's not – Filipino. Get loads of 'em here – mostly tarts and hostesses. There are probably as many of them in the country working on the sly as there are us English teachers.'

A figure strode into view ahead of them. There was a familiarity in his walk. As he stepped out into the light of a streetlamp, Daniel saw the soft outline of Mr Chiba. He recognized Daniel and faltered.

Daniel was also unsure what to do. He felt awkward at having been seen in such an area and had no desire to begin a conversation. But to ignore the man completely might cause more trouble. It would be insulting. Best to give a brief greeting without stopping.

But Mr Chiba walked stiffly past, staring ahead as if his eyes were fixed in place.

'What was up with him?' asked Jake.

'That was Mr Chiba. His wife runs the school.'

'Weird guy. He looked as if he had a carrot stuck up his arse.'

'I wonder what he was doing here so late. Sometimes he parks the car in these streets, but then why pretend he hadn't seen me?'

'He's probably just got his rocks off with some poxy tart – didn't like being caught out.'

Jake led Daniel through to a low doorway; above it was a sign, weakly lit, that read 'Manhotton Bar'. Behind was a broad but dingy room filled with wooden tables and chairs, but no customers. The walls were decorated with large but faded photographs of Switzerland, just penetrating the gloom. There was no air conditioning and the atmosphere was oppressively hot.

'I thought you said this place had character,' said Daniel.

'It certainly did last time I came. You just wait.'

They sat down at a table. A solitary waiter padded across, none too pleased to see them. He pointed to his watch to say the bar would close in less than an hour.

'Dismal bugger aren't you?' said Jake. 'Just bring us some beer.'

The man shuffled away.

Daniel peered round the room. At the darker end he made out a complex sound-system, including microphone, speakers, and rack upon rack of tapes. The only other noticeable feature of the bar was a raised platform, on it a long table, two dozen or more chairs placed around it. Already it had been laid out with glasses and chopsticks. Daniel guessed it was for some large party.

The waiter struggled back with two bottles of beer, opening them with some reluctance.

'Thanks mate – you're a real treasure.'

They had extracted two more bottles from the waiter,

and Daniel was beginning to doubt Jake's claim that the bar had 'character' when the door swung open with a bang. In walked a large woman, scantily dressed, her face hard and unsurprisable.

'I knew they'd turn up,' said Jake triumphantly.

Another had followed her in. The first shouted a greeting to the waiter, who looked nervous, feigning laughter. Seeing the two westerners, she turned to her companion and made some remark. The second woman glanced at them and let out a shrill conspiratorial giggle.

'Looks like they reckon we might bring 'em some trade,' observed Jake, pleased.

A third woman walked through the doorway behind them, then another, a fifth and more. Daniel watched as the room became filled with their shouts.

'It was just the same the last time I came here,' said Jake. 'Must be a regular after-work drink – comparing notes on the evening's customers.'

'But they're huge – I've never seen Japanese women so big.'

'Their customers must like them that way. Either that or it's the beer they get through.'

In amongst them Daniel noticed an office worker in a blue suit. With them he floated up towards the banquet table, thin and buoyant, smiling with improbable inno-cence. The whores ignored him, being more concerned with the evening's gossip, but he was unbothered. Reddened with alcohol, his face was blissfully relaxed.

'Spot the wanker,' said Jake. 'Must've been one of the last of the evening's customers. Surprised they let him tag along.'

At the end of the table sat the woman who had first entered and who had pointed them both out. She seemed to hold some authority over the others. It was she who ordered the drinks and was now clapping her hands to hurry the waiter to bring them beer and snacks. Seeing the westerners watching her, she winked and curled her tongue out of her mouth.

'Come over here – we're waiting for you,' Jake shouted up to her. He raised his glass in a toast and greedily swigged the beer; some of it trickled down his beard. 'Look at those thighs and tits – really something to get hold of, eh?'

'They're disgusting,' said Daniel. 'I can't understand how they get any customers.'

'No need to get all snotty about 'em,' said Jake crossly, as if Daniel was scorning his taste in women. 'They've got a hole in the right place and that's the main thing.'

There was a slight hush at the banquet table. The office worker had stood up and was talking slowly and earnestly, as if making an after-dinner speech. The women watched with expressions of derision as he made his way round the table to the chief whore. He bent down to speak in her ear. With some nervousness he took her hand and led her down from the platform to the corner with the microphone and speakers.

'He just wants to sing,' said Jake, disappointed. The audio system amplified all too clearly his thin, hopeful voice. As the song progressed, his tone became discordantly passionate and he slipped his arm as far round the waist of the chief whore as he was able.

Standing with legs slightly apart, like a boxer, she yawned. Then, glancing towards the westerners, she walked away towards them, leaving the office worker stranded in mid-song, his arm flopping back to his side.

'We're in luck Brit,' said Jake.

'You are – not me.'

She drew up a chair, but leant against it rather than sitting down. 'You are American boys?'

'I'm from Australia – down under.'

She turned to Daniel. 'And you?'

'English.'

She gave him a glance of curiosity. 'You are teacher – near here teacher?'

Daniel nodded, puzzled by her interest.

'Yes,' she announced. 'I like teacher.'

'We both are,' broke in Jake. 'English teachers. But that doesn't mean we're against doing a little learning ourselves – perhaps even some Japanese lessons.'

She ignored him and turned to Daniel. 'I sit down?' It was an announcement rather than a question.

'Go ahead,' replied Jake. 'Make yourself at home.'

She turned to find a chair.

'Let's get the bill,' said Daniel. 'I've had enough of this place.'

'Stop being such a bloody pom.'

Daniel glanced at his watch. The last train had gone. And he doubted he had enough money for a taxi all the way back to Takasago. He should have realized something like this would happen. 'You really want me to stay?'

'Of course.'

If Daniel left now he would not be able to crash out on Jake's floor. He decided to bide his time, for the moment at least. 'All right. But I don't want to be too late.'

The chief whore was back, with not one but two chairs – she had also brought her companion. For a moment Daniel hoped he might get away with talking with the latter, who seemed the quieter of the two women. But the chief whore soon made her preferences clear.

'I want to sit with English man. I like English.'

'Your lucky day Brit,' jeered Jake.

She sat next to Daniel, winked at him, then turned to shout to the waiter to bring them more beer.

Daniel peered at the photographs of Switzerland. The gloomy light and years of accumulated smoke had transformed the colouring of lakes, fir trees and snow to various hues of brown.

The beer had arrived. The women poured for all of them, the chief whore then raising her glass into the air.

'Foreigners – foreigners in Zudanuma. *Campai.*' She shot Daniel a glance. 'Foreigners and Japanese together.'

There was a crash of steps outside the door and three businessmen rolled in. They seemed to know the bar well – one shouted a greeting to the main body of whores, then all three hurried down to the gloomier end of the room, to the sound system.

'They sing,' explained the chief whore to Daniel. 'You like Japanese song?'

'I can't say I do.'

There was a loud thump as the amplifier was switched on. After a brief excited discussion the three businessmen selected one from a caseful of tapes, all backing tracks to popular Japanese songs. Standing behind the microphone, arms on each other's shoulders, they began droning in unison.

'You like Japanese girl?' asked the chief whore.

'Some of them,' replied Daniel warily.

'I think you do.'

'Is that so?'

'I know.'

There was a squawk from her companion. She had decided Jake was doing too much too quickly for her liking – he had one arm round her shoulders while she had just removed his other hand from her thigh, where it had been freely roving.

'Don't be such a kill-joy,' he complained.

The businessmen had finished the song and two had sat down, but a third remained standing to begin a ballad, passionate and of great length.

The chief whore leant closer to Daniel, so that she was touching him. He breathed in her smell – a sour, sweaty smell.

'I know you,' she murmured.

The drone of the singer, the clink of glasses, the shouts of the whore, all sounded suddenly jarringly sharp. He could not understand how he had come to be in such a place.

'Stop trying to wriggle away.' Jake's voice rose above the din. 'What are you here for if it's not for a bit of fun.'

The face leered closer to Daniel's. Even in the poor light he could discern the overdone make-up below her eyebrows – purple and black.

'You have Japanese girlfriend?'

'What if I do?'

'You do – I know it.'

'And how do you know?' Daniel thought he saw a triumphant look in her eyes, as if enjoying some advantage he was unaware of.

She stuck out her tongue. 'I know nothing – maybe. But your girlfriend – I think she is older than you.'

'What d'you mean?' demanded Daniel.

She laughed, delighted at his discomposure. 'Nothing – maybe.'

He stared at her, trying to detect if she really knew something, or if the whole conversation had been based on no more than a malicious guess. How could she know?

She leant closer to his face. Through Jake's shouts and the wailing of the businessmen he heard her words again. 'I know you. I know you and your girlfriend.'

'What the hell are you trying to say,' he shouted. 'How do you know her?'

She drew back with an awkward laugh, as if she had gone too far.

'Tell me.'

'Joke,' she explained. 'Joke for English. Only joke.'

She could not know. Or could she? Suddenly Daniel had had enough of the noise, the smoke, of her smell. 'I'm going.' He stood up.

'Eh?' said Jake, taken aback. 'But we've hardly started.'

'Maybe you have; I've finished.' He called over the waiter. The ground seemed to be swinging slightly beneath his feet – the effect of the drink.

'Why you go?' demanded the chief whore coyly. 'You not like me?'

The waiter scrawled the bill on a piece of paper. It came to six thousand yen. An extortionate amount, and Daniel knew it. But he was not prepared to stop and argue.

'Six thousand,' he said to Jake. 'Three each.'

'Come off it. You don't really want to go now.'

'Three each,' Daniel repeated.

Jake took out his wallet and began leafing through it very slowly.

'You stay,' suggested the chief whore. 'Finish beer. Talk with me.'

The companion nodded. 'Talk.'

Daniel remained standing.

'Hell.' Still very slowly, Jake began searching through his pockets.

'Something wrong?'

'I must've left it back home – that ten-thousand note. And I was sure I'd brought it.'

'How much have you got?'

'Just a few coins.'

'You stay,' repeated the chief whore. 'Talk with me.'

Her words decided Daniel's mind as nothing else could have done. To pay would leave him with just one thousand yen, but that was better than staying longer. He banged the notes down on the table and walked out.

Through the entrance and into the street, quiet now, with most of the bars closed and empty. He felt refreshed by the calm, even by the rain on his face.

He had gone only a few yards when he heard footsteps tapping urgently behind him. It was Jake.

'Why d'you have to walk out on me like that?'

'Walk out on you?' Daniel was astonished by the tone of reproach in the Australian's voice.

'Us foreigners gotta stick together. It's not right to scram like that.'

'Oh yes?'

'Yeah. You knew I only had a couple of coins to my name, and you left me high and dry.'

'For Christ's sake, I paid the bill. What more d'you expect?'

'Us foreigners gotta stick together,' repeated Jake accusingly. 'I was doing great with that bird. But how am I gonna get anywhere if I haven't a yen in my pocket.'

Daniel noticed the change from past tense to present. 'You mean you expect me to lend you some? You've got to be joking.'

'What's the big deal? I've got the cash back home.'

'Then go and get it. I haven't got any here.'

'Nothing?'

'It all went on that last bill.'

'You're sure?'

'Quite sure.'

'That's just great,' said Jake bitterly. 'One ruined evening.' He spat angrily on the pavement. 'And I was really looking forward to it. Thanks Brit.'

'Don't try and blame me!' Then Daniel remembered that he was hoping to sleep on Jake's floor. 'You can't have been that worked up,' he said slowly. 'She was as ugly as hell.'

'She was all right.'

'Okay, she was Miss Tokyo, now let's get out of here.'

'All right,' agreed Jake reluctantly. 'After letting me down like that I reckon the least you can do is give me somewhere to crash out.'

Daniel stopped. 'Somewhere for *you* to crash out? You mean you don't live round here?'

' 'Course not,' said the Australian with a touch of scorn. 'I don't live anywhere – don't like the idea of paying some bastard rent. At the moment I'm holed up with some Yanks, way across the other side of town.'

'That's just fine,' growled Daniel. 'So where am I going to stay now? If I'd known you didn't live round here I would have made sure of catching that last train.'

Jake turned slowly towards him. 'You don't live round here either?'

'No. My place is this side of Tokyo but it can't be less than ten miles from here.'

'Great, eh?'

They stood for a moment, glaring at one another. A gust of wind caught the rain and whisked drops into their faces. Jake was the first to speak. 'Got enough for a taxi?' he asked.

'I told you already. I'll have to hitch a ride.'

The Australian nodded grimly. 'Yeah, that's what we'll have to do.'

'We?'

'Come on mate, how long d'you think it'll take me to hitch all the way across Tokyo – sodding hours.'

'You should have thought of that earlier.'

'What about you? You were quick enough to think that I'd put you up.'

Daniel had to admit he had a point. He gave a reluctant nod. 'All right – come on.'

They walked towards the nearest main road. Daniel noticed how Jake was staggering slightly as he walked. Nor was he the only one. To Daniel all objects seemed to have a misty coating to them – it was as if he was viewing them through a grimy window.

Traffic on the main road was sparse, mostly travelling in the wrong direction; they waited some time before a car stopped. The driver was friendly and eager to help two stranded foreigners, but his route passed a couple of miles from Takasago; he was in too much of a hurry to take them on such a long detour.

'It's all right,' said Daniel. 'We can walk the last stretch.'

The rain had stopped by the time they left the car. They made their way into the maze of silent streets, shoes clacking noisily on the wet pavement.

Daniel was grateful for the sight of a familiar water tower rising up in the distance. It was when they had just passed the landmark that he felt the ground shifting gently beneath his feet. At first he thought it was the effect of the beer. Then he heard the rattle of window-panes all around him.

'It's only a tremor,' said Jake.

'First for ages.' Daniel thought of Keiko. Many of his students, especially the schoolgirls, had told of how frightened they were of earthquakes. They knew what havoc they could cause. Keiko was particularly affected, and would burst into tears at tremors that Daniel was barely aware of.

They walked on. A light rain began to fall around them. Beyond the water tower the roads became more confusing, overcrowding Daniel's sense of direction. It was some time before they stumbled across his street. Glancing down it Daniel saw his apartment, the lights on.

'That's odd – there must be somebody in there.'

'Probably your bit of fluff.'

'But it's so late. Maybe she was in earlier and left the lights on.'

'Something wrong Brit?' asked Jake cheerfully. 'Anybody'd think you wanted to keep her hidden away from your mates.'

Up the stairway. Daniel opened the door and breathed in the stale steamy air. He was hardly inside when Keiko tripped towards him, clutching him by the waist.

'I am so frighten.' Her face was red with crying.

'What's wrong?'

'Earthquake. I run from my house and there is nobody here. But now you are come.' She looked round, startled by Jake walking in behind him.

'Don't mind me – I'm a mate of your boyfriend here. The name's Jake.'

'Jake's from Australia,' explained Daniel awkwardly.

'That's right. And a great place it is too.' He paused to examine Keiko, grinning approvingly at what he saw. 'So this is the cause of all the trouble, eh? You didn't say she was a looker.'

She stared at him, alarmed by his appearance and baffled by his strange English.

'You can sleep here,' said Daniel, determined to cut him short before he could say something harmful. 'There's no spare mattress but there are a couple of cushions.'

Jake was not so easily silenced. 'You in a hurry or something? I've only just stepped in the door – haven't even been properly introduced to the lady.'

'I thought you must be tired.'

'Well I'm not.' The Australian turned to Keiko. 'Friendly, isn't he? First he doesn't want to put me up – prefers the idea of me spending all night out in the rain. And when I am here he doesn't so much as offer me a drink. I can't understand what you see in such a bloke.'

She looked at Daniel, uneasy at the confrontation she saw brewing.

'Come on,' he told her. 'It's time we got some sleep.' He turned to Jake. 'You may not be tired but I am.' He led her through to the bedroom.

Jake followed.

'There he goes again,' he complained. 'Trying to drag you off against your will.'

'It's not against her will,' said Daniel angrily. 'She's as tired as I am.'

'I wouldn't get yourself hitched up to such a pommy kill-joy if I were you,' Jake continued. 'You'd be better off heading down under – lots of great blokes there who'd be happy to take on a looker like yourself.'

She asked Daniel anxiously, 'Looker?'

'I think you ought to leave us alone,' said Daniel quietly.

Jake shot him a glance. 'Imagine spending your life with a stuffy pom like that,' he observed to Keiko. 'No, you'll be better off if there's no baby.'

There was a jarring silence.

Keiko stood very still. She looked from one to the other. 'No baby – what do you say?'

'Will you get out of here?' demanded Daniel of Jake. 'I don't know what the hell you think you're up to.'

'Doing you a favour – I thought you wanted her to know.'

'Not like this.'

'What do you say?' repeated Keiko.

'This isn't the right time,' urged Daniel. 'I'll explain it all tomorrow, when we're alone.'

She turned to Jake. 'What do you say?'

The Australian shrugged his shoulders. 'All right – you'll find out soon enough anyway. Your boyfriend wants you to have an abortion. He's even willing to pay for it.'

'Abortion?'

'Will you stop?' demanded Daniel.

'Can't keep her in the dark now, can we? Doctor come,' he explained, miming what looked like a maniac armed with a pair of shears. 'Doctor come and take out baby. Baby all dead.'

She shot a glance at Daniel to see if it were true.

'He's not saying it right,' he protested. 'The idea is good – it's the only solution. He's just not saying it right.'

'I must speak with my father,' she said slowly. She turned and went out of the door. Daniel hurried down the stairs after her. He caught her up.

'It wouldn't have been any kind of life for us. It wouldn't have worked. Don't you see?'

She began walking briskly towards her home.

'I didn't mean to tell you like this – it's all wrong. Let me walk you back and explain.'

'No – I go alone.'

'It's important.'

She gave him an angry look. 'It is better that you are quiet now – or it will be more bad.'

Daniel watched her march away.

Slowly he walked up the stairway. Jake had cleared a

space for himself to lie down and was using the two cushions as pillows.

'What the hell did you think you were doing?'

'A favour to you mate,' drawled the Australian. 'Saved you having to pluck up courage and tell her yourself.'

'I think it's time you left.'

'Sorry mate – I don't much like the idea of dossing out in the rain somewhere.'

'All the better.'

'You gonna make me go?'

Daniel saw from his eyes that he was willing to fight over the issue, perhaps even looked forward to the prospect of a scrap. He felt sickened. As if it mattered – the damage had been done.

Chapter Five

Daniel dreamt that he was ill. He was searching for something on the ground, but found his movements hampered by aches throughout his body. His left arm felt lifeless and numb.

There was also Mrs Chiba. She was clinging to his back, digging her heels into his rib cage. She could be placated but only with huge gooey sweets. These should have been in Daniel's pockets. But rummage as he would, he was unable to find any – his hands felt nothing except a sticky film. And the telephone was ringing.

He opened his eyes and found that he really did feel ill. He was lying uncomfortably on his left arm, which was lifeless and numb.

The telephone rang again. He lay still, listening for it, waiting for the next ring. His thoughts contained a residue of alarm left over from the previous night. He remembered enough to wonder if it was Keiko's father calling.

He heard it ring again, imagining the receiver shifting slightly on its hook. It occurred to him that if he did not answer it, her father might pay a visit in person. He climbed up from the futon, room gently swimming around him. Pushing open the door to the bedroom, he reached towards the telephone. It fell silent.

He glanced round the room. A pile of cushions, Vital text-books, and Daniel's dirty washing heaped into a form of mattress marked where Jake had slept. There was no sign of him.

Daniel's movement from the bedroom had stirred his system into the beginnings of activity – a dull rhythmic ache began behind his temples. He found it hard to think clearly. It was as if his thoughts were glued to each other. Only one amongst them rose out clearly, insistent and repetitive: he had to eat.

There was almost no food in the apartment – there never was. He found three eggs and decided to make an omelette. Breaking the eggs into a tea-stained mug, he added milk, seeing too late that the liquid had separated into layers. He smelt it – on the very edge of going off.

Still he cooked the mixture. He fried it too quickly, so that some parts were blackened while others remained liquid. The absence of salt gave it an oddly sweet taste. But having cooked it, he ate it, and felt worse than before.

He put the plate and pan in the sink, turned on the tap, and was watching them cover over with oily water when he heard a series of strange bangs and heavy steps on the stairway outside, as if he were being visited by a hugely cumbersome animal.

There was a sharp rapping at the door. He opened it and ducked out of the way as Masayuki lumbered inside, a sharp-faced uncle just behind him, both bent beneath the burden of a shiny white fridge.

'What's that for?' demanded Daniel.

They stumbled to the far side of the room and carefully deposited the object in the corner.

'Why have you brought this?'

Masayuki unwound the flex and connected the plug into a nearby socket. The machine responded with a low whirr.

'Present,' he said.

'But I didn't ask for it. What if I don't want a fridge?'

Masayuki shook his head dismissively. 'Father come later.'

'You can't just leave it there.'

Masayuki seemed to disagree. He and the uncle strolled out of the door. Daniel watched them climb into a van parked below.

They did not drive away but waited until another figure stepped out into the street and climbed inside the vehicle. There was no mistaking the man's thickset build – it was Masayuki's father, Mr Harada. And Daniel was almost sure he had watched him come out of the doorway of the next-door house – his landlord's house.

He looked at the fridge. It whirred back at him. Opening the door he found that it was full, shelves well stocked with packets and cartons. He recognized some as the ingredients Keiko put in her soups.

He had to do something; anything was preferable to sitting, waiting. He would try and contact Mrs Chiba and settle with her about the money he was owed – at least that would be a start. He picked up the telephone, hesitated, then replaced it. Better just to go straight to her house. He searched his pockets and found easily enough coins to take him to Zudanuma.

The train was crowded, even on this, a Sunday. He stood through the journey, still feeling uncomfortably weary from the events of the night before.

Staring through the window, he was acutely aware of the ugliness of the landscape, as if he had never fully noticed it before. Every building seemed to have been constructed with no thought for its appearance, only for earthquake regulations and cutting costs. The city did not even have the distinction of being grotesque – only unremittingly plain.

And the people. He looked at the other passengers, dozing or staring at the floor, expressions blank, thinking of their companies, the unpaid overtime they had just worked. It was as if they had acquired tunnel vision, an inability to see how they were living.

He could not stay in such a place.

As he walked from the station, he tried to ready himself for the coming argument, to imagine and counter Mrs Chiba's evasions. He felt so worn out.

It was she who opened the door. Her face showed surprise – perhaps at his unexpected appearance on her doorstep, perhaps at his face.

'What is happen? You are ill?'

'No. I have to talk with you – it's very important.'

With a suspicious look, she ushered him into the alcove to remove his shoes, then on through to the sitting-room. The television was on; she turned down the sound but left it flickering.

'So what do you want to tell me?'

'It's about the question of money. I know we've talked about this before many times, but something has happened. Suddenly it's very important that I have all the wages owing to me for the last few months – four hundred thousand yen.'

He expected indignation, a cry of 'Money, money, with you it is always money.' But she sat still, very quiet. 'All?'

'Yes, all of it. The school's doing well now. I'm sure it must be possible.'

Still no explosion. 'For what reason you need?'

'I'm afraid I really can't tell you. It's personal – a private matter.'

'I see.' She stood up. 'Please wait. I must talk with my husband.'

Still baffled by the calm of her reaction, Daniel waited, watched by the silent television – a chat show, with guests and presenters vying with each other's smiles. From deeper in the house he heard the wail of the baby daughter.

The chat show ended, replaced by a bloodthirsty Samurai soap opera, before Mrs Chiba returned. She sat down, face grave.

'There is nothing else you want to tell me?'

He tried to guess what she was fishing for. Keiko? 'No. Nothing.'

'You are sure?'

'Quite sure.'

She nodded thoughtfully. 'I must talk with bank and arrange. In one week we can settle all.'

Daniel could hardly believe what he heard. 'A week? You'll pay it all in a week?'

'A week on Monday – it is okay?'

'Yes, I suppose . . .' Daniel was in no state to think through his reply. He was like a man who throws his full weight against a door he believes locked but which then flies open, leaving him sprawling through onto the ground.

'And for now – you have money?'

'Hardly a yen.'

From a small rubbery purse she took a brown 10,000-yen note. 'Here – for the one week.'

He took it from her. At last his sense of suspicion began to revive – if she was so happy to settle matters now, why fight so hard before?

'You're sure this'll be all right?' she asked. 'Monday week?'

'Sure.'

★

The sky darkened as he walked back to the station; a rain-cloud was sweeping overhead. Sharp gusts of wind blew as he waited on the platform, rattling the station signs that hung from the eaves above. A brief flash was followed by a rumble of thunder, not far away. The deluge began, silencing the crowded platform with its clatter, and raining spray onto those huddled along the edge.

The train crept into view, windows misty with condensation. Daniel managed to win a place standing by one of the doors. Now that he appeared to have settled matters with Mrs Chiba, he had to ponder more seriously how he should try to convince Mr Harada that an abortion was the best solution. The more he thought, the less optimistic he became.

It was still pouring when he got out at Takasago, and he was quickly drenched. Despite this, he slowed down his pace as he neared his home, glancing through the rain for any sign of the Haradas' car or van. He crept cautiously up the stairway, peering round the door as he opened it.

The apartment was empty, just as he had left it, except for the gentle shuddering of the building in the wind, the clatter of the rain on the roof. From the corner the fridge whirred softly.

He stared at it. Then scoured through the flotsam on the low table and extracted his address book.

When he arrived he had had the numbers of several westerners living in Japan. Of these, he was certain that all had left except one, an Irishman whom he had met while travelling, last heard of living several hundred miles from Tokyo.

He rang the number. A shrill woman's voice answered in Japanese. He asked for the name, Sean O'Rourke. Her voice became all the more shrill, confused by the foreign words.

'Sean O'Rourke,' he repeated. She hung up.

He dialled again, this time the international operator – there was no direct dialling abroad. A young girl took the name and number of a girlfriend Daniel had known briefly just before he had left England. A moment later, through a fog of hums and clicks, he made out an accent he had not heard for a long time – South London, refreshingly bored.

'Lunnun what?'

The number rang in reassuringly familiar double bleeps, not the single tone of Japan. It rang and rang. Daniel was beginning to lose hope of an answer when the line clicked.

'Yes?' she drawled crossly.

'It's Daniel – remember me?'

'No I don't.'

'I'm ringing from Japan.'

'Oh, you. If you have to ring, can't you pick a better time? It's not even six yet, and on a Sunday morning.'

He had forgotten the time difference. 'I'm really sorry – I didn't realize. And I had to talk with someone.'

'Oh did you?' She was not placated.

'You see I'm . . . It's not easy to explain.'

A pause. 'Why don't you ring back later?'

'No, no – please, you don't understand – everything's getting out of hand here.'

'Then come home.' She did not sound hopeful that he would.

'It's not so simple.' Daniel faltered. 'You see there's this girl.'

'Is there?'

'And she's pregnant.'

'You have been busy,' she said tersely.

'I just don't know what to do.'

'And you want me to tell you, do you?'

'I didn't mean . . .' he began. 'I just wanted to talk to someone.'

'And now you have. And you'll have to sort this all out by yourself I'm afraid.'

The conversation was almost ended. Daniel cut in before she could complete it and say goodbye. 'Listen, can I ring you back later, when you're not so tired?'

'I think I'd rather you didn't.'

Daniel held the receiver, listening as the line clicked back to the dialling tone. He could not hang up now. He again rang the international operator.

'England please. This number – it's in Sussex.'

'Name you are calling?'

'Mr Thayne – my father.' He would be awake, even so early on a Sunday morning; he always rose meticulously early. Sure enough, only after a couple of rings a dry voice answered.

'Hello – who is this?'

'Daniel – it's Daniel.'

'He's not here. He's been away for more than three years.'

'No – I'm Daniel. Your son.'

There was a long, long pause. 'Yes.'

'I know I should have written or rung before now – I'm really sorry,' Daniel began. 'But so much was going on. And after I'd left it a while it became more difficult. I didn't know where to start.'

'Your mother's been very concerned.' The voice seemed to echo, as if in a huge empty room. 'I'm surprised it hasn't affected her health.'

'I'm sorry, I really am.'

'You know she has trouble with her liver.'

Silence.

'I'm in Japan now – living here. I've found work

teaching English. I've got an apartment in Tokyo. In fact I've even got a girlfriend here – Japanese.'

'Japan?' his father said at last. 'We hadn't realized you'd gone so far.' His tone implied reproach for the distance covered.

Daniel was thoroughly regretting his decision to make the call; he was suddenly frightened that it would turn into a row. 'I meant to write before and tell you about everything here. But there's been so much going on. The girl – the one I'm seeing . . .' It was hard to talk of Keiko to his father, like using obscene language. 'You see, her parents are concerned.'

'So are we.'

'Of course. But you don't understand . . .' Then he blurted out the words. 'She's pregnant.'

'I see.' Silence. 'I'll have to tell your mother. I don't know how she'll take news like that.'

'I'm in trouble for Christ's sake. I don't know what to do.'

'Now don't start raising your voice at me,' retorted his father.

'Can't you see? Things are out of control here.'

'I don't understand you at all. We don't hear a word out of you for all this time and you ring suddenly with all this bad news, and you start bellowing at your own father.'

'I'm not bellowing.'

'I don't know what your mother would think if she knew of this outburst. It might affect her health.'

'I'm sorry.' Daniel tried to calm himself. 'I didn't mean to shout.' He wanted only to end the conversation as quickly as possible; he felt he could not go on for much longer. He might lose his temper again. 'Listen, I have to go now.'

'Don't you want to speak to your mother?'

'I think it might be better if I didn't.'

'I can wake her.'

'No, don't. Just send her my love.'

'She'll be very disappointed, not having heard for so long.'

'Sorry, I've got to go now. I'll speak to you sometime later.' He hung up before his father could fit in a further objection.

He replaced the receiver and sat down on the floor in the very centre of the room. He remained there, quite still, while above the roof of the house the weather shifted and changed.

The tapping of raindrops slowed in tempo and the sky lightened to milky grey. Later, gusts of wind rattled the windows in their panes, announcing the approach of another storm. Cracks of thunder; sporadic lightning, illuminating the deluge. The sky lightened once more in a short interlude between storm and dusk. Another steamy night began.

Daniel did not move from his place on the floor. All lights off, the room was lit only by the pinkish glare of streetlights, shining in through the windows.

A car drew up outside. He listened as the doors slammed shut, heard Mr Harada's voice bark out an order, his two sons chanting back in acknowledgement. The metallic clang of steps on the stairway, gently shaking the whole house. And a harsh rap on the door.

Daniel heard his name called out, sounding so near that it could have been a voice inside. He said nothing.

There was the click of a key in the lock and Mr Harada stepped into the room. He switched on the main light.

'Why do you sit in the dark?'

'Why not?'

'It is bad that you do not answer the door.' His two sons

followed him inside, together with one of the sharp-faced uncles. The three of them remained silently just inside the doorway.

Mr Harada sat down opposite Daniel. 'Your behaviour is not always good,' he observed gravely. 'Yesterday you are too drunk with your . . .' He frowned at the word, as if it tasted bad. 'Your friend, Australia man. And today you sit in the dark and do not open your door. You must be careful – your behaviour must be better for the arrangements.'

'What arrangements?'

'Arrangements I have made. Marriage arrangements.'

'I haven't agreed to any marriage.'

Mr Harada narrowed his eyes in surprise at Daniel's complaint. 'Hotel reservation is for Sunday – seven days from now, just after national holiday. Very good hotel.'

'But I haven't spoken with Keiko. I haven't been consulted at all. I am involved.'

'You want to leave her alone with your child?'

'Of course not. But Mr Harada, think how hard it would be. If we stayed in Japan, the child would never be fully accepted as Japanese. In England Keiko would find herself a stranger. And the marriage itself – would it work? There's the language problem. And the ages. I'm seven years younger than she is. It would be much better if . . .'

'Impossible,' said Mr Harada softly.

'I'm not trying to evade my responsibilities. I know the gravity of what's happened. There's only one way I can see of showing how seriously I take the whole matter. I'll pay for the operation. It may sound crude and tactless, but I can see no other way of helping.'

Mr Harada's eyes settled on Daniel's in a slow stare. 'Impossible,' he repeated. 'For the doctor.'

'You mean medically – she can't have an abortion?'

'Yes – not possible.'

'You're sure?'

'Of course.'

'But how did you find out?'

'Not important.'

It was a moment before Daniel was able to take in the full weight of what he had heard.

'So you must be careful of your behaviour,' Mr Harada resumed. 'You must not be like Australia man – we do not like him in Japan. You must think of guest to wedding – your family if you like.'

'Yes,' said Daniel dumbly.

'And employers at language school.'

'Why does it have to be so soon?'

'It is best – for baby.' Mr Harada stood up, surveying the room with a glance. 'I think your house is a little dirty – not modern. Tomorrow my family will come here and make improvement.'

'But what if we don't want to live in Japan?'

'Later we can talk of that – after the marriage.'

Chapter Six

Daniel had been deeply asleep when they first arrived.

He had left the bedroom door slightly ajar in the hope of a breeze. Through it he watched a bizarre procession as it entered. Keiko's mother led the way, quite changed from the meek person she had been at the family lunch. As the matter now at hand was wholly domestic, she was in command. She turned to her two sons, lumbering in behind her beneath the burden of a new bath, and instructed them where to place it.

Next came a plumber, arms filled with a bouquet of tubing, piping and tools; Mrs Harada pointed him towards the bathroom. Bringing up the rear of the procession was Keiko, head bowed, as if it was not a wedding that was approaching but a funeral.

Daniel looked at his watch. It was barely eight in the morning.

He watched them, wondering if he was expected to help. It was not as if he had asked them to change his home.

He dressed and walked out of the bedroom. The tiny flat was already filled to bursting with commotion. The two brothers were enthusiastically clearing furniture to one side of the sitting-room, while from the bathroom came a hammering sound as the plumber set to work disconnecting the old, leaky bath. Daniel approached Mrs Harada, directing operations from a commanding position by the front door.

'D'you want any help?'

She shook her head busily. 'No – we are enough.'

He stood, watching the activity all around, then crossed to Keiko, idling by the cooker.

'Any chance of some tea?'

'Of course.' She filled the kettle.

Daniel surveyed the room. 'It's going to look quite different here.'

She nodded.

'Are you pleased?'

'Yes – very please.' She fidgeted with the packet of green tea.

'And you're happy with the plans for the wedding?'

'Happy – of course.'

'You don't look as if you are.'

She emptied the teapot of its damp, blackened tea leaves. 'No, very happy.'

'Keiko.' Her mother called her over, instructing her to help lay dustsheets on the carpet. 'Please,' she offered, taking Keiko's place at the cooker. 'I will make tea for you.'

The van arrived, bringing Mr Toshio and the sharp-faced uncles, as well as wooden trestles and pot after pot of white paint. The trestles barely fitted in the sitting-room; nor were they necessary as the ceiling was easily reachable by standing on a chair.

Daniel began to wonder how far the 'improvement' of his apartment would go. He decided to confront Mrs Harada.

'I'm not sure you can do all this,' he explained. 'At least you should consult my landlord first – he might object.'

Mrs Harada gave him an impatient look – she had other matters to attend. 'No, I think different.'

Daniel felt she had not understood. 'All this – the man who owns the house may say no.'

'No, not important. Please, my husband is here soon.'

Reluctantly Daniel returned to the bedroom – there was no space for him in the other room. He sat on the futon, listening to the thumps and bangs next door, until the telephone rang. He made his way back through the commotion and picked up the receiver.

'Hello, Danieru? Hello?'

'I'm here.' He held the receiver close to his mouth to try and keep out the sounds of the Haradas' work, but without success.

'What are your noises?' asked Mrs Chiba.

'Some work next door.'

'I see. Well, you must know very bad news. Vital School air conditioner is break.'

'It hardly worked before.'

'But it is big break – much work indeed, very noise. So my husband is decide to close school for one week.'

'Close the school? Surely that's not necessary.'

'No, very necessary – too big noise.'

'But for a whole week?'

'Very big repair take long time.'

'I see. And what about our agreement over the wages – that's all right?'

'No change. But do not visit the school for this next week – all close and also I think dirty. Very important.'

Daniel decided to go and see for himself.

Mrs Harada saw him pick up his jacket to leave. She shouted to Masayuki, stooping on the trestle.

'Where do you go?' he called down.

'Private lesson,' Daniel replied, annoyed by the question. 'Why do you ask?'

'Okay, you go.'

Rain-water was streaming down the walls of the department stores of Zudanuma. Daniel stopped just outside the station to peer up at the solitary window of the school. There was no sign of life.

Up the stairs, past the hamburger restaurant, dentist and Japanese Chess Centre, to the school itself, metal door adorned with a large poster in Japanese and English.

'Vital International Language Institute. Good international experience now for you today. Good.'

He slipped his key into the lock and pulled open the heavy door. Inside it was dark. He felt for and found the light switch and glanced around him. Mrs Kamakura's desk had been cleared of stationery and was now dotted with metal parts. On the floor was the beached hulk of the air conditioner. He began to wonder if he was losing all sense of judgement.

He explored each classroom, searching for anything unusual. All was exactly as he had left it after finishing his last lesson; even the writing on the main blackboard was untouched.

As he made his way back towards the reception area, he heard a sharp tap of footsteps rising up from the bottom of the stairwell. There was no mistaking the distinctive brisk clip. It was Mrs Chiba.

He plucked up a copy of the school textbook and sat behind the desk. The steps grew nearer, quickening when she reached the final flight and saw the door was open. As she marched in and saw Daniel, her face fell into surprise and annoyance.

'Why are you come here? I tell you not to come — school is close.'

'I wanted to borrow this textbook — help me plan some future lessons.'

She nodded, unconvinced. 'It is better you do not

come again – repair men will be here. I came to talk with them but they are so late.' She shook her head. 'Very bad.'

Daniel took the textbook and went, but not far. He spent the best part of an hour in a hamburger bar, sitting by the window, watching the entrance to the building that housed the school. Amongst the few people whom he saw enter were two men in overalls, each carrying a toolbox. The repair men.

He had to change trains on his journey home. As he reached the platform, he heard a squeal of wheels and saw the silver snout of a 'Skyliner', an express that covered the twisting route through the suburbs, without stopping, on its way out to the airport.

There must have been some congestion on the line ahead. The train edged alongside the platform at a walking pace. Daniel looked in through the windows at the passengers. Most were Japanese, but there were a good few westerners amongst them: businessmen, tourists, students, teachers. He caught the distant look on their faces – in their thoughts they were already halfway to their destinations.

The ceiling and walls of the sitting-room were being cleaned when Daniel returned, the dust of years suddenly made visible in huge grey swirls. Mr Harada stood observing the change.

'You are back from lesson,' he said as a form of greeting to Daniel. 'Far?'

'Not far.'

'Difficult lesson? You are away long time.'

'There was a lot to do,' said Daniel briefly. 'But what I wanted to talk to you about was this decoration. I think you ought to check it's all right with the landlord, the man who owns the house.'

Mr Harada gave him a quizzical look, as if puzzled by such a pointless request. 'All arrange,' he replied. 'Everything arrange.'

'You've spoken with the landlord?'

'Of course. I arrange to buy this house from him.'

'Buy it? But why?'

'It is good house – quite near station. Good home for Keiko and you.'

'What if we want to live somewhere else?'

Another quizzical look. 'Later we talk. Now I am busy with work.'

He dropped in several times during the day, checking on how the redecoration was progressing. Already he had given Daniel's number as one where he could be reached. The phone rang several times for him during the afternoon.

By evening both the main rooms had been cleaned, while the sitting-room had a fresh coat of white paint. Keiko and her mother cooked dinner for those present, although there was barely room for them all to sit down to eat. Mr Harada returned just as the bowls were being cleared away.

'Now I must arrange marriage party,' he explained to Daniel. 'What guests do you invite? Employers at language school?'

'No, they can't – they're going away.' Daniel was reluctant to invite anybody as it would seem as if he accepted the wedding as a definite event. The thought of announcing it to Mrs Chiba was particularly unappealing.

'And your family?'

'They also can't make it – it was too short notice.'

Mr Harada nodded solemnly. 'Very pity. You will

have no guests.' He glanced around the room. 'And so much work, so small time. But Masayuki and Kunio,' he indicated his eldest son and one of the uncles. 'They will help – they stay here this night to make early start.'

'Early start? They really don't have to – I can help out tomorrow myself.'

'No – you must not,' insisted Mr Harada. 'Work is present of my family. They insist.' He called out to Masayuki, who set about hauling up two futon from the van below. He and the uncle laid them both down by the front door.

'They haven't left themselves much room,' said Daniel. 'If someone walked in suddenly they might step on them.'

'It is their choice,' answered Mr Harada. 'They have less smell of paint.'

Certainly there was no shortage of paint smell – the whole apartment was filled with the stink of it, strangely merged with the residual aroma of Keiko's cooking.

Lying in the steamy darkness, Daniel was uncomfortably aware of it, as he was of the breathing of the two Haradas, just by the front door.

When he woke he found them already up, sipping tea and talking in short bursts of gutteral conversation. They seemed in no hurry to begin work, doing nothing until the others arrived.

It was that day that Mr Harada took Daniel to visit the wedding hotel.

Toshihiko drove, this time wearing no shades. They approached central Tokyo by motorway, much of it a flyover, passing high above the squat offices and shops. As they dropped down into the landscape, the hotel came into view. Daniel saw a couple step out of the entrance, dressed in full western costume, behind them an entourage of guests.

'Many wedding here,' said Mr Harada approvingly.

He was greeted fulsomely by one of the reception clerks, who lost no time in leading them up to the two rooms where the event was to take place: one for the ceremony itself; another for the dinner that followed.

Mr Harada took Daniel through them both. It was to be a formal wedding in the modern fashion, a mixture of Japanese and western styles. The ceremony itself was Buddhist – mainly a matter of bride and groom drinking special sake from three cups placed within each other, like Russian dolls. Keiko would wear a traditional kimono, Daniel a sober grey gown, while the guests would be carefully selected relatives.

The dinner, held a few doors away, would include a large number of guests. Speeches would be made – flattering descriptions of both parties. The event would be western, with French food. By this point both Daniel and Keiko would have changed into western wedding clothes.

The thought struck Daniel that he could not go through with this. He tried to imagine what Jake would do. Certainly he would get out of it somehow, without qualms of conscience. And he would be far too cunning to be caught without money or passport. But then did Daniel want to be like him?

'Very pity that you have no guest,' continued Mr Harada, now explaining the dinner-room. 'Mr Toshio will make speech for you – there must be speech – as if you are in company. Other guests are all in company.'

'All of them? Your whole family?'

'Of course.'

'Just what kind of work do they do?'

Mr Harada gave him a disapproving glare for having asked such a prying question. 'Company work.'

'But what kind of company is it?' Daniel persisted.

'Business company.'

'What sort of business?'

'Company business.'

By mid-afternoon the sitting-room had received its second coat of paint and work had begun on taking up the green carpet. The material was thin and tore easily, releasing a cloud of small green tufts of fluff into the air.

In the midst of the commotion the doorbell rang. Opening the door, Daniel found himself looking at Samuel Echtbein. He peered suspiciously around the room.

'You moving out?'

'No – quite the opposite.'

'Who are these guys?'

'The family of the girl you saw me with the other night.'

'Oh yuh?' Echtbein was not convinced. 'I'd like to have a chat with them.' He hobbled across to Mr Harada.

Daniel watched them as they spoke, in Japanese, testily trying to extract information from one another. Echtbein was the first to drop his guard, face slowly relaxing as his words began to flow more freely. Then the caution lifted even from Mr Harada's face. Echtbein proffered his hand and it was shaken.

He hobbled back to Daniel and slapped him weakly on his back. 'Hey – congratulations. Now I really can say welcome to Japan.'

Work on the carpet had already halted as those involved vented their curiosity on the unexpected guest. Mr

Harada called for a break and instructed Keiko to make green tea.

'We must celebrate happy moment. Very lucky. Now we have wedding friend for Danieru – Mr Echtbein is agree to make speech for him.'

They sat around the low table, sipping the green liquid, all silent except Mr Harada and Echtbein. It was Echtbein who did most of the talking: a gush of conversation. Mr Harada broke in with a few low, unhurried comments; to each of these Echtbein replied with keen nods of his head.

'Hey, we gotta do more to celebrate this,' he said to Daniel when the tea was drunk. 'After all, looks like we're gonna be real neighbours now. Whad'ya say we head over to my place and you meet my family. You might even pick up a few useful ideas on living here.' He glanced at his watch, then grinned at the devilish idea that had occurred to him. 'I know it's only five-thirty, but we could even break open a can of beer.'

Echtbein lived only a few hundred yards away, in a house very similar to the one that contained Daniel's apartment. Sitting at the kitchen table, listening to Echtbein talk at length of Hoovers and rice cookers – he was a born teacher with a passion for explaining – Daniel began to regret having accepted his invitation.

'You'll be amazed at how much trouble a rice cooker'll save your new wife. And the way it works is real simple . . .'

His own wife bustled behind him, preparing snacks. From a next-door room came a succession of bangs and screams. The three sons were watching cartoons on the television.

On the table between Daniel and Echtbein stood a solitary beer-can – Echtbein's offer to 'break open a can of beer' had been quite literal. He had given them both particularly small glasses, so that it would last several pourings.

Through the windows Daniel saw a plump dog staring inside, stubby legs pressing against the glass. He cut into Echtbein's monologue on rice cookers.

'Is he yours?'

'Sure is.' Echtbein forgave the interruption since, after all, it paved the way for a whole new line of explaining. 'He's a traditional breed, indigenous to Japan.'

Daniel nodded. 'He seems to want to come in.'

'Well Dan, that's something else you'll have to know about, if you ever think of keeping a pet here. You see there's not much point in us all taking our shoes off at the door if you have animals walking in and out, bringing in dirt. So you have to settle either for an inside animal or an outside one.'

'I see.' Daniel sipped his beer and found he had drunk it all.

'Because the house is kinda like a shrine.'

It occurred to Daniel that Echtbein's knowledge of the country could be of some use to him. 'D'you know much about Japanese companies?'

'Some, I guess.'

'Is it usual for a whole family to work for the same one?'

'Sure, nothing strange in that. A lot of people marry someone in their company.'

'Wouldn't it be a little odd for a whole family to take several days off work – at short notice.'

'Might be hard to organize – why d'you ask?'

'The Haradas seem to have as much free time as they like. And Mr Harada was very unwilling to say what kind of company it is, though I get the impression that he owns and runs it.'

Echtbein frowned. 'What are you trying to say?'

'I'm not sure. But there's something unusual about the family. And they seem to be watching me all the time. It's hard to get away from them.'

'Hey now – that's not true. They're just worried that you don't know how things work over here. I hate to say this Dan, but I really don't like to hear you running them down like that.'

'You've barely met them.'

'I've been in this country a while longer than you have Dan,' said Echtbein in a slow, patient voice. 'I guess I know a few things you don't.'

His wife placed the snacks on the table. As she leant past her husband, Daniel noticed how much healthier she looked than he did.

'There's an awful lot you've got ahead of you to learn,' Echtbein resumed, in a forgiving voice. 'You haven't even begun to tackle the language – speaking, let alone writing.' He began describing the complications of the writing system, the intricate combination of the two alphabets and several thousand characters. The monotone in which he spoke was beginning to get on Daniel's nerves.

'Of course, if you really want to learn you'll need lessons,' he continued. 'In fact I could probably fix you up with some at the college where I teach. I'll look into that.'

'It's kind of you but please don't bother.'

'It's no trouble.'

'You don't understand – I'm not sure I want any.'

Echtbein looked puzzled. 'You must have lessons – you'll find it real tough to learn without.'

'I'm not even sure I'm going to stay here. I think I'd rather not.'

'Both leave?' Echtbein was quite taken aback. 'But what about your apartment, the decoration?'

'I've warned Mr Harada that we may not stay. If he wants the apartment redecorated anyway, that's his decision.'

'But you'd be crazy to leave. I don't think you realize how lucky you are. This is the country of the future.'

'Then perhaps the future isn't for me.'

It did not take them long to finish the beer and snacks. Echtbein saw Daniel out.

They passed through the room where the three sons were watching television. In the cartoon on the screen were a dog and a bear, both wearing suits, involved in a violent gun-battle, darting up from behind dustbins to blast each other with machine guns. The cartoon homed in on the barrels of their guns, bullets pouring out, then on their faces, contorted with rage.

'You like this?' Daniel asked the eldest son. He looked up, uncomprehending. 'Good programme?'

'It's his favourite,' Echtbein answered for him.

Daniel did not hurry back, despite the rain. He took a roundabout route, alongside the railway, and stood for some time by the tracks, watching housewives cycle over a crossing, coloured umbrellas held precariously above their heads, and the trains as they rumbled past.

'Still so much to do,' observed Mr Harada. His family were cleaning up for the end of the day. A new carpet was in place, while a new and larger cooker had been installed.

'It is best that my two sons stay tonight – for early start.'

'Early start?' said Daniel. 'But when Masayuki and your brother stayed over last night they did nothing until you arrived. There was no need for them to be here.'

'Is it true?' Mr Harada coughed disapprovingly. 'So lazy. I will talk with Masayuki that he works hard.'

'It's really not necessary; there'll be enough time to get everything done.'

'I am not so sure. And it would be too sad if house is not ready. Of course if it is inconvenient – if you hate my sons – then it is different.'

'I didn't say that.'

'Good – then all is correct.'

When the others had gone, Masayuki, in slow heavy movements, laid the two futon on the floor, in the same spot where they had been the night before, just by the front door.

Toshihiko began examining Daniel's possessions, picking up one of the slide boxes. To Daniel's anger, he plucked out a slide with his finger and thumb, touching the transparency itself. A greasy fingermark could damage it.

'Put that down,' Daniel called out.

'What is?'

'Put it back,' Daniel shouted. 'You'll ruin it.'

Puzzled rather than put out, Toshihiko replaced the slide and instead began examining Daniel's cheap Walkman tape-player.

'You have American music?' He seemed disappointed when Daniel said he had none. 'Then we go for drinking – saloon.' With his hand he swung an imaginary glass and watched it spin to a halt along a huge film-set bar.

His brother was unsure. But Daniel was happy to get out of the apartment. His support decided the issue.

Toshihiko led the way, out into the warm air. He stopped not far from Daniel's house, at a traditional bar – no hostesses here, nor even an audio system, just row after row of identical bottles, each containing the same colourless liquid. A character or two scrawled on the glass indicated the regular customer for whom it was reserved.

Toshihiko was apologetic for the drink available. 'No whisky here – I am sorry that only shochu.'

'Shochu good,' grunted his brother.

They sat along the bar. Toshihiko took the middle place, excluding Masayuki from the conversation. He talked excitedly of American music, mainly a long list of names.

None too pleased at his isolation, his elder brother repeatedly leant round Toshihiko to refill their glasses, then shouting '*Campai*' and raising his own. He insisted on each occasion that they drain all the vodka–like spirit.

Before too long Toshihiko's face began to colour with a reddish flush. His words slurred, so much so that the American names peppering his speech became less and less comprehensible.

Daniel interrupted the string of rock groups. 'D'you like your work, for your father?'

'Work, job,' he agreed rather distantly. 'I like.' He broke into song. 'I like to be a rock star.'

'What sort of work do you do?'

'Big work – too big. No time for music.'

'What kind of big work?'

'Work work – no fun,' Toshihiko noted bitterly. 'I like western girl – you like?' He laughed before Daniel could reply. 'You must – you are western. So – you like Japanese girl?' He laughed again. 'Of course – you like Keiko.'

Masayuki glanced round at the name. Daniel could see him straining to decipher the conversation.

'But Japanese girl is too small,' Toshihiko continued, cupping his hands as if he had two breasts. 'Small here. You don't hate?'

'No, I don't hate.'

'That is good,' observed Toshihiko, suddenly practical.

'And my sister like western men very much – eyes, hair. She like westerners.'

'Westerners – you mean there were others?'

Comprehending just enough to sustain his suspicion, Masayuki gave his brother a warning nudge. Toshihiko turned scornfully to him.

'You are the crazy man – crazy, crazy, crazy. You do not understand – nothing. Electric train – you understand it?'

Ashamed at his ignorance, Masayuki stared angrily down at the bar.

'Stoopid man.'

Daniel resumed. 'There were other westerners?'

Toshihiko pointed to Daniel's face. 'Eyes, bright hair – he is like you.'

'But who was he? Her husband?'

Toshihiko let out a cackle. 'Not husband – opposite of husband.'

'But she was involved with him?'

'Western man is singing man, guitar man. I like electric guitar . . .' Toshihiko's concentration was lapsing – he seemed not to have taken in the question. Daniel was determined to extract the truth.

'The other westerner,' he demanded, 'was he Keiko's lover?'

He realized his mistake at once. He had oversimplified the words. Masayuki had understood. He lumbered off his stool, crossed to his brother and hauled him up by his collar, in the process spilling glasses and bottles behind the bar. The sudden commotion silenced the other drinkers. The barman shouted out for him to stop.

Whining with incomprehension, Toshihiko was dragged out of the building and flung against a rainy wall outside. His brother gave him a noisy slap, then another and another.

'Stop hitting him,' demanded Daniel. He tried to pull Masayuki away but was himself flung back. The elder brother struck Toshihiko again, then propelled him back towards the apartment, barking rebukes and pushing him onwards throughout the walk.

Toshihiko had gone before Daniel woke.

Work resumed as before: Mrs Harada directing events from her vantage point by the front door, her husband frequently dropping in for short visits of inspection. The telephone seemed to be ringing all the time now, always for Mr Harada.

No mention was made of the events of the previous night – it was as if they had not occurred. Daniel decided against confronting the parents with the question of the other westerner – they would simply stonewall him. Better to wait for a chance to talk to Keiko alone.

The bedroom was cleared, cleaned, and given its first coat of fresh white paint. Eventually Toshihiko returned. He walked past Daniel, studiously ignoring him, and set to work.

Daniel kept a close watch on Keiko. She was fitting curtains. Wherever she was standing, her uncle or elder brother always seemed to be close by.

After lunch the task was begun of replacing the tatami rush mats that covered the floor of the bedroom. As the old ones were taken up, it soon became apparent that many of the floorboards beneath had rotted.

'More work, less time,' complained Mr Harada. It was decided to call in a carpenter.

On his next visit of inspection, Keiko's father was faced with a further setback. He was called to the telephone, where he spoke for some time. Afterwards he relayed the news he had heard to his family, then to Daniel.

'More delay. Worker of my company in hospital is sadly dead. Tomorrow is his party and all my family must watch – of course not you. But it is less time – we must work so hard.'

Tired of watching, Daniel began repainting the bathroom. With the new urgency over the redecoration, Mrs Harada offered no objection.

It was evening, and he had almost completed the room's first coat when a chance presented itself. In his determination to ensure that all was completed in time for the wedding, Mr Harada had insisted that they all worked later than usual, even the carpenter. The hammering of new floorboards into place was unavoidably noisy, seeming to shake the whole flimsy building. Before long there was a knock at the door. It was the downstairs neighbours, people Daniel had barely met before.

Mr Harada went into the front room to talk to them. Daniel glanced across at Keiko busily fitting curtains in the bedroom, but her elder brother was close by, as well as the carpenter.

The chatter at the front door continued – it seemed Mr Harada was determined that the work should go on. The carpenter was called out from the bedroom to give some sort of evidence. A moment later Masayuki succumbed to curiosity and marched out to watch how the dispute would end.

Daniel walked across to Keiko. 'How're you doing?'

She jumped slightly at the sound of his voice. 'All fine.'

'I've hardly had a chance to talk to you for days – is anything wrong?'

She smiled awkwardly. 'Nothing wrong.'

'Nothing?' He raised her chin so that she had to look at him. 'Last night your brother talked of another westerner you knew.'

'He is too much drunk.'

From outside the room Daniel heard her father's voice lecturing the downstairs neighbours; already he had won the upper hand in the discussion.

'There must have been more to it than that – when Masayuki found out what he was saying, he attacked him.'

'Nothing.'

'I must know.'

She looked up at him, full in the face. 'No – you must not know. It is better for you.'

'Why better?'

'More safe.'

Daniel was alerted by a new silence. He heard the front door shut and turned just in time to see Mr Harada step into the tiny room.

'Why do you shout at my daughter?'

'I'm not shouting at her, I'm talking to her. Anything wrong in that? After all, I am going to marry her in a few days.'

'I think your talk is wrong.'

'Wrong? I just wanted to find out what's going on here – what Toshihiko meant by talking of another westerner.'

'He means nothing. He is drunk. He is behave also a mistake.'

'Just a mistake – then why did Masayuki hit him?'

'Because he is too drunk – he is incorrect.'

'I know there's more.'

Mr Harada fixed him with a slow stare. 'You say I am a liar?'

'No, I . . .'

'It is better that you do not say.'

Gusts of wind were rattling the windows in their frames. The work on the apartment was almost complete: the new tatami mats were laid, the curtains were in place, and a new front door was being fitted. A sheet of thick transparent plastic had been tacked outside the doorway to prevent the rain from blowing in.

Mr Harada glanced at his watch and announced, 'We must go to the dead man's party.'

He waved to his family to collect their raincoats and umbrellas.

Daniel watched them as they filed across the road, drops of rain bouncing from the stretched cloth of their umbrellas. They stood by the car, waiting while Mr Harada climbed inside.

Mr Toshio stood watching while the workmen attached the door. He was staying, ostensibly to ensure that the work was done properly.

Across the road all the Haradas were now inside the car and a trickle of smoke was visible from the exhaust pipe. The machine was ready for a sedate journey across Tokyo, as was proper for a funeral.

It was then that Daniel saw him. Stationary beneath his umbrella, half-concealed round a corner, he was also watching the Haradas. There was no mistaking his stiff way of standing, the way he held his umbrella as if it was enormously heavy. It was the man with the squint.

The Haradas' car pulled out and slowly drew away. Then, to Daniel's surprise, the man looked up at the apartment window, straight at him. He glanced about him, then waved for Daniel to come down.

Mr Toshio was still standing by the doorway, watching the carpenter. Startled, he tried to block the exit as Daniel pulled up the plastic covering.

'Where you go?'

'Out.'

'But Mr Harada . . .' The confusion on his face gave

him away. Daniel slipped past him and down the stairway, listening for steps behind him. There were none. Still, he did not stop when he reached the man with the squint, but walked past as if he did not know him, round a corner, out of sight of the apartment.

'I am sorry for disturb you,' said the man as soon as he had caught him up. 'But I am worry for you.' He waved his hand towards where the car had been. 'You know these people?'

'Of course I do.'

'Then I must tell you that it is better that you go from here – that you leave Japan.'

'Why?'

'These people are not normal – they are not like Japanese.'

'But how'd you know?'

'Through my work.'

'At the bank?'

'No, no,' he said impatiently. 'At Immigration Office.'

Daniel was baffled by the admission. 'How do you know the Haradas?'

'Not important – not now.'

'But what is it about them that's so dangerous?'

'I tell you, not important,' said the man angrily. 'Only important is that you leave at once.'

For a moment Daniel wondered if the whole business could somehow be a bluff to make him admit that he was working illegally.

'Why don't you just deport me?' he asked.' You work for Immigration. I'm telling you now that I've been teaching English without a visa. I'll even give you the address of the school where I'm teaching.'

'No, no,' said the man, almost despairingly. 'Not possible. You are lucky I tell you – now you must only go.'

'It's not so easy – I can't just walk out. Their daughter – I'm supposed to be marrying her.'

'Marry?'

'Yes, in just a few days. You see she's pregnant. My child.'

Now it was the man with the squint's turn to be baffled. 'Why don't you tell me before?'

'Does it matter?'

It seemed that it did. He bowed his head. 'I am sorry to disturb you. I must go.'

'But you can't – you've told me almost nothing.'

'There is nothing. My mistake.' He turned away. Daniel jumped after him, only to have the other throw his umbrella in his path, tripping him.

By the time Daniel had picked himself up the man was already round the corner, climbing into a car. Daniel thumped on the windows, without effect – he accelerated away.

Bowls were on the table, steam rising from the food within them. A hum of chanting voices recited '*Ita dekimasu*'. Keiko held out the largest bowl to her father and he scooped rice onto his plate. The muffled clicking of wooden chopsticks began.

Mr Harada chewed some food thoughtfully, then asked Daniel, 'Your school – do they call you?'

'No, not yet.' Daniel had spoken hardly a word all evening. He wondered if they had noticed.

'Not good.' Mr Harada frowned concern. 'Maybe they are not such an excellent school – it is not reliable to close so much.'

'They'll open again on Monday.'

Mr Harada nodded, unconvinced. 'Many worker in my company want to learn English. If you like you will teach them – it is better that you work for company of your new family.'

'It's very kind of you to offer,' said Daniel slowly. 'I'd like to think about that very carefully.'

'Of course.'

Daniel swallowed more beer from his glass. 'The funeral – was it all right?'

'Dead man's party. Yes, it was good,' said Mr Harada blankly. 'And of course sad.'

'The company worker – was he young?'

Mr Harada gave him a warning look. 'Normal age.'

'But what did he die of?'

'Accident – only accident.'

Chapter Seven

The pace of work had slowed down almost to a standstill – Mr Harada had overestimated the need for urgency and there was now very little to do. Toshihiko, still pointedly ignoring Daniel, was fixing up a high shelf on which would be placed a small shrine to the house. The apartment was emptier than it had been for days – Keiko and her mother were out shopping for extras for Keiko's wedding costume, while Masayuki was buying some cupboards for the sitting-room.

Mr Harada saw Daniel pick up his jacket. 'You go out?'

'Yes – private lesson.'

The plumber was back, now to replace the sink. He had switched off the water supply for the day while he dealt with a problem with the pipes. Even the toilet would not flush; somehow Mr Harada had convinced the downstairs neighbours to let his family use theirs.

'Please wait for moment,' he said to Daniel. 'My son will take you in the car.'

'I really don't need a lift. And he's working.'

'He wants to drive you,' Mr Harada explained. 'And it is raining very much. If you walk then I think you may become sick for the wedding – very bad.'

Daniel put on his jacket. 'It's not at all far.'

'Family?'

'Yes – friends of Samuel Echtbein.'

The mention of Echtbein's name had a calming effect on Mr Harada. 'You are back soon?'

'An hour or so.'

'That is good.'

Daniel began walking through the steamy drizzle, towards the station. The man with the squint's warning had done nothing to clarify matters, serving only to add to his sense of alarm. He had so little room for manoeuvre. Most of all he needed money.

He stopped at a telephone box to call Mrs Chiba's home. After all, she had agreed to give him what he was owed only the next Monday. A couple of days should hardly matter to her.

The number rang and rang. No reply. He decided to make his way direct to the school – he might catch her there.

But glancing up at the solitary window he saw no sign of life. As he climbed the stairway, he saw the door firmly closed. No sign of any repair men, let alone Mrs Chiba.

From his pocket he took his key. It would not turn in the lock.

He felt he must have the wrong one – the key to his apartment was very similar. But when he tried the other he found it would not even fit in the socket. He tried the first once more, but with no greater success. The lock had been changed.

It was possible that there had been some accident and that the old lock had been damaged, perhaps some mishap connected with the repair of the air conditioner. But why had she not told him? Mrs Chiba usually plagued him with every petty detail of the school.

He turned and made his way down the stairway and out of the building. Past the rain-swept walls of the department stores. The mournful electric chime sailed down to him. Through the swirling traffic and beyond the railway line to the far side of Zudanuma.

The road twisted and into view came the Chibas' house. Daniel thought he saw a flicker of motion in one of the windows, as if a curtain had been slightly drawn. By the time he reached the door all was still. He rang the bell, rang it again, but was answered only with silence.

He walked away, but not far — just out of sight around the corner. There he waited, ignoring the curious glances of passers-by, who wondered at the sight of a westerner loitering so obviously.

The rain clattered on the pavement around him. It soon permeated his jacket hood and began to dribble down his forehead. He was beginning to wonder if he had really seen any movement in the window — he had been some distance from the house — when he heard the sound. Barely audible through the rain, but there was no mistaking it: the angry wail of the baby daughter.

He pressed the bell once more. The wailing stopped. He banged his fist on the door. Silence. Stepping back, he shouted up to the windows, 'There's no point in hiding away inside there. Why don't you just show yourselves?'

Quiet.

'You can't shut yourselves away for ever. I know what you're trying. I'll be back.'

He slowly turned. He thought of Mr Harada's eagerness for him to start working for his 'company'. He would have to regain his place at Vital somehow. He would return.

He stood on the station platform, waiting for the train to Takasago.

An unshaven, ageless-looking man pushed his way through towards him. His clothes marked him out as a tramp: a well-worn coat and a strange peaked cap that might once have belonged to a yachtsman. He stopped only a few inches in front of Daniel, staring at him. Surely he could not be connected with the Haradas as well.

'What d'you want?' Daniel was surprised by the loudness of his own voice. Faces turned.

'*Namae,*' croaked the tramp. He brandished a card, holding it close in front of Daniel's eyes. On it was printed a picture of a warship. Daniel wondered if it had something to do with the last war.

'*Namae,*' repeated the man '*Namae,* addlessu.' He proffered a stubby pencil.

Daniel scribbled his name and address on the back of the card, eager to get rid of the man. Satisfied, the tramp pressed the card into a wallet that was bursting with them, all waxy with use. He stumbled away.

As if such a man could really be linked to his other troubles. Daniel felt a twinge of alarm at having thought of it.

The train drew alongside the platform, windows grey with condensation. Daniel clambered aboard. As the stations passed by, the carriage began to empty and he was able to find a seat, opposite two schoolgirls who were flipping through a book together, squealing with giggles at each page.

The train halted at a station, delaying for a few moments. Through the open doors floated the howl of a dog, suddenly, as if stung.

As the train moved off, Daniel twisted round in his seat and with his sleeve rubbed a porthole in the moisture clinging to the window. Through it he watched the succession of houses fall away and vanish, their place taken by the girders of the bridge over the River Edo – grey water beyond, with rain rippling the surface.

Not far to go. There was a station just past the bridge,

one more and then Takasago. Daniel felt the carriage rocking as it slowed. Must be high winds out there. It promised to be a foul walk back to the apartment.

The girders flashed past less and less frequently as the train slowed. It drew into the shelter of the station, but the rocking did not end, it increased. The doors slid open and in rushed a chaotic uproar of clatterings. Daniel saw the station signs swinging overhead like bells, striking the eaves from which they hung. A typhoon? But the rain-drops were falling as straight as stones. There was no wind at all.

One of the schoolgirls shrieked. Daniel tried to stand up, his sense of danger at last alerted.

He lunged to grab one of the steel supports – the carriage was pitching and rolling like a ship. He was just able to haul himself towards the doors.

Outside he saw two women trying to climb the stairway to the platform, clutching the steps to prevent themselves being thrown back down. The carriage came alive around him as everybody stood up at once and struggled for the doors.

As people spilled out onto the platform, the rocking of the train became less frantic. The tempo of the signs' clattering slowed. The two women were able to stand up and reach the platform.

Amongst the crowd collecting beside the train there was a moment of quiet, a group recognition of danger passed.

Then a burst of chatter and talk, nervous laughter, excited comforting of those still crying. A railway official barked an announcement and the train's engine whirred in readiness to complete the journey.

The streets of Takasago were more crowded than usual. From the people's excitement Daniel guessed that the earthquake must have been a particularly strong one.

Housewives and children lingered uncomfortably in the rain, unwilling to return to their houses for fear there would be a second, more destructive tremor. The few who had ventured back leant out of upper windows, shouting out what damage they had found, eager to keep in close touch with those below.

Here and there was evidence of destruction, mostly slight: a toppled pyramid of tins outside a shop; roof tiles that had slipped and smashed in the road.

As he walked through the district Daniel felt a light-headedness, a result of the novelty of the event, the surprise and relief he had shared with the others on the train. He felt almost as if he belonged. As he watched people hurrying past, he wished he had the language to stop and talk with them.

Close to his apartment he reached more severe damage. A mains water pipe had cracked and unleashed a small river of liquid. Near by was a block of flats, the lowest of which was at basement level and had already half flooded.

The family and neighbours were doing their best to ferry valuables up to the safety of the flat above. Daniel joined them, carrying sections of a stereo, a cupboard, even the family shrine. Before long a fire engine arrived and guzzled the water away through a grimy fat hose. The housewife shook his hand warmly. He moved on.

From the outside he could detect no damage to his own apartment, although he was surprised to see the front door hanging open, swinging in the light breeze. Walking up, he found it very much as he had left it. The family shrine was still on the floor, tools scattered around it. There was no sign of the Haradas.

He switched off the gas main tap. He did not need to worry about the water as that had already been discon-nected by the plumber. He decided to inspect the apartment, just in case there was some damage he had not spotted from the outside.

The sitting-room was unscathed; the only evidence of the earthquake was a whisky bottle that had toppled from the desk, without breaking. The bedroom lacked even that much. But in the bathroom there was a hairline crack running from the ceiling to the floor.

He turned to the lavatory, the one room he had not examined. Pulling open the door – seated, head in her hands – he found Keiko.

'What on earth . . .'

She looked up. 'Go from here. Leave me.'

He looked away. He would have shut the door and left her, but something delayed him – a faint scent in the air, barely sensed, slightly sickly.

'What are you doing here?' he asked.

'Earthquake,' she answered curtly. 'I run here from house, and there is nobody.'

'Why hide away in here – you must have heard me?'

She gave no reply, but stood up. Pulling off several sheets of lavatory paper, she wiped herself, then quickly pulled her clothes back into place. She pulled the lavatory handle but it did not flush.

It was then that Daniel caught a familiar, overripe odour, a mixture of decay and perfume. He reached for the door handle.

She pushed it shut. 'You must not know.'

'I want to see if there's any damage.'

'No.'

He pulled open the door. Then stood, trying to make sense of what he saw. The liquid in the bowl was coloured a deep scarlet.

She looked at the ground.

For a moment he imagined she had been hurt. Her

behaviour said otherwise. Slowly he understood. 'It was a lie,' he said quietly. 'The whole thing was a lie. But why do it?'

'My father says I must do it,' she mumbled. 'For you.'

'For me?' He took her shoulders and shook her. 'There never was a baby. You never were pregnant. But why do it?'

She spluttered into sobs. 'I am so shame.'

'Why?'

'My father is so anger.'

'What have I done to him to make him angry?'

She bowed her head and he shook her again and again. 'I've had enough of being in the dark – tell me.'

She reached her hand in front of his eyes to stop him. 'Please – I tell you.'

He realized he was hurting her and relaxed his grip.

'First I say nothing to my father of us – it is secret. But then you are different – so cold. I think you hate me. I am fright you will go away. One night I call my father and tell. Then I know I am wrong – I call you at the school. But I cannot say to you.'

'And your father?'

'He says he is not angry. He says I must tell you there is baby. I said it is bad to lie – I cannot. But he says all westerners are lie – we must lie too. And if you know there is baby then you will change to better person with more heart, not so much foreigner. Still I think it is bad to lie. But I do not say.' She gave a sudden shake of her head. 'But then I see that you do not become more heart – you are more cold and sad.'

'There's more to it than that, I'm sure of it,' he insisted. 'Otherwise why should he go to such lengths to try and see us married?'

'Nothing more.' She buried her face in his jacket.

He pushed her back, so he could see her face. 'There's something – I know there is.'

'Maybe small thing,' she admitted. 'Long time ago. Four years before now I live as housewife, near here. My husband works for big electrical company. He is very clever and works hard. Soon after wedding he goes to Germany for two years for working.

'I have very much time. I like to drink coffee with my friend from school and her boyfriend – she has romance with American man who is teacher like you. But romance end. American man call me and say he wants to see me. I say no, it is wrong. But he calls again, says only meet, and – I am bad. It is my fault.

'My husband finds this. He is so shame – marriage ends. My father is very angry – I say it is my fault but he says no, it is foreigner.'

'And what happened to him – the American?'

'He is gone – leave Japan. But my father will not forget these things. When I tell him of you he says you may also be like the American. You must be made to behave correctly – to change the bad happening to the good.'

He scrutinized her face, watching for some sign of whether her last story was truth or invention. Her tear-stained eyes showed nothing. And what she had said fitted well enough with what her brother had given away, that there had been another westerner.

He glanced at the front door. 'Your family – where are they?'

'I do not know – they are gone when I come here.'

He guessed they were probably checking for damage at the company site; they could return at any time. He was not ready to face them, not until he had talked with somebody who could help him understand what was happening. A westerner. But he knew none he could reach. A moment's reflection and he corrected himself: there was one. And he claimed to know enough about the country.

He turned to the door.

'Where do you go?' asked Keiko.

'Out.'

'Please – I will come with you.'

'No, I'm going alone.'

She bowed her head. 'You hate me?'

'I didn't say that.'

'Of course you hate me – I know. And you are correct.'

'If you think so.' He walked out through the door, only to hear the footsteps behind him. 'I told you – I want to go by myself.'

She said nothing. But when he walked on she followed, three steps behind, the traditional style for the obedient wife. He stopped. So did she, three paces behind.

'Why are you following me?'

'I want to show you that I am sorry.'

'Fine, you've shown me. Now go back.'

She nodded, as if accepting his demand. But when he began walking, she did too. He was losing patience. He had to lose her – for all he knew, she might be spying for her father.

'You want to make me happy?' he asked.

'Of course.'

'Then go home – that'll make me happy.'

'I am worry for you.'

'I don't want you to worry.'

'You hate me so much.'

'All right,' he said wearily. 'Yes I do – I hate you so much. And I'll hate you even more if you don't go now.'

'I see.' To his relief she turned and began walking slowly away.

He watched until she was quite out of sight. Only then did he make his way onwards, through the streets to Samuel Echtbein's house. He rang the bell and soon heard the owner's irregular step.

'Hi Dan. What brings you here?'

'Can I come in?'

'Sure.' Echtbein stood back to give him room to remove his shoes. 'You've come at the right moment – I've just finished my speech for your big day.'

'Right – that's . . .'

'It's only a couple of days off now, right – are you nervous?'

'Well . . .' Daniel ran dry – there was too much to explain at once. He followed Echtbein into the house. 'A lot's changed since I last spoke with you.'

'Oh yuh?'

'I've found out that they were lying to me – the whole family were lying. Keiko wasn't pregnant after all.'

Echtbein frowned. 'I didn't know she had been.'

'They didn't tell you?' Daniel had presumed Echtbein had known. 'Well they told me – it was a device to push me into marriage.'

'Oh yeah? I thought you wanted to marry her.'

'Well – I thought I had a duty to because she was carrying my child.'

'That so?' Echtbein tapped the table surface with a chopstick. 'I still don't understand why they should lie to you.'

'I'm not clear on it all myself. There was another westerner who Keiko had been involved with before – I'm sure it's all to do with that.'

'Another westerner, huh?'

'That's not all – there's also the man with the squint. He visited me saying he worked for a bank – I got the idea he was checking up on me. And yesterday he appeared and warned me to leave the country – he said the Haradas were dangerous.'

'A squint. How does he fit into all the rest?'

'I just don't know. The second time he came – when he warned me – he said he worked for Immigration.'

'And how does he know the Haradas?'

'I just don't know.'

Echtbein smiled a thin smile. 'I hate to say this Dan, but I get the idea that there isn't much you do know.'

'That's why I need your help.'

'Uh-huh. Well, perhaps I'd better tell you what I know. I know that from the very start you were really shy of doing the right thing by this girl you'd gotten involved with. I'm afraid it has to be said – you're frightened of taking on responsibilities.'

'You don't understand – these people are up to something. They were lying to me. I don't know what it is that they're involved in, but it could be dangerous.'

'Listen Dan, I've met this family – they're a nice bunch. And I've lived in this country long enough to know that things just don't happen the way you've described . . .'

'They have.'

'Hey – let me finish. I think you need to be a little more realistic in the way you view things here. Try to see matters as they really are . . .'

'But I do.'

'Will you let me finish? You asked me for help, and I'm willing to give it. I'll try and sort matters out between you and Keiko's family, work out what's really going on. I think the best hope is if we all got together and talked it through.'

'No,' said Daniel suddenly. 'I'm not going to talk to these people until I know just what they are.'

'Don't you think you should at least try to be reasonable?'

'I am.'

'Well, I'm afraid I'm just not prepared to let you walk out on this family.' Echtbein reached towards the telephone. Daniel pushed it away.

'I was wrong to come here.'

'Now look Dan.'

'No – I think I can well do without your help.'

Outside it was growing dark. Feeling the rain on his head, it occurred to Daniel that he had given no thought to where he was going. From habit rather than any chosen plan he began retracing his steps back to his apartment. The lights were on.

He stood for some moments below the building, catching glimpses of shadows flickering against the windows. He wondered what they could be doing, what Keiko had told them.

He knew what he should do. He should go up the stairway and confront the family with their lies. He should order them out. And if they would not go – they did after all own the building now – he should take his slides and cameras, things he could not leave behind, and clear out.

He looked up at the shadows flickering against the windows. He was scared.

He tried to imagine what he would say, how he would begin his attack. He thought of the warning look that he would see on Mr Harada's face, of Toshihiko being hurled against a rainy wall and slapped by his brother. And he thought of what the man with the squint had told him: 'These people are not normal. They are not like Japanese.'

And he knew he could not go up.

He turned away from the stairway and began walking.

He felt sick at himself but still he walked on. Towards the station. He had to get away from Takasago. He would stay the night somewhere, anywhere. And the next morning he would go to the British embassy for help.

He took a train into central Tokyo and began walking through shopping streets, still crowded with office workers on their way home. Flipping through his wallet he found what was left from the ten thousand yen that Mrs Chiba had given him – not enough for a room at even the cheapest hotel. He would sleep out.

He walked through to a large shrine much visited by western and Japanese tourists. It was already closing – along the avenue of souvenir stalls, shutters were being clattered into place, while a priest was locking up the huge chest into which coins were thrown for prayers.

Daniel sat at the top of the stairway leading to the shrine, and waited until he had the place to himself.

He watched as the rain fell on the tarmac all around. Ten days before he would have found it hard to imagine himself sleeping rough in Tokyo, exiled from his own apartment.

He lay down beside what looked like a huge bronze tulip, of some religious significance he did not comprehend. Folding his arms into the nearest he could manage to a pillow, he began the task of trying to sleep.

Chapter Eight

Daniel woke as dawn was breaking, and knew he would not be able to catch any more sleep – he was too uncomfortable. The air felt chilly. He had curled into a ball to try and keep warm. One leg and one arm ached from their prolonged contact with the wooden boards of the shrine.

He clambered stiffly to his feet and began walking. The streets of central Tokyo were quite deserted – not a car, not a figure was in sight. It was as if he were the only one awake in the whole country.

The rain had stopped. Somewhere behind the thick skin of clouds, the sun was rising. The air quickly changed from clammily cold to clammily warm. Outside the moat of the Imperial Palace he found a small patch of open green, a rarity in central Tokyo. He lay down in the damp grass, waiting for the time to pass before the embassy opened. He was soon dozing.

He woke with a start, to the sound of a bus rumbling past. Glancing at his watch he saw it was after nine. But the roads were still all but empty of people or traffic. He began walking, soon reaching a station. One old man limped out of the entrance; normally there would be a constant stream of commuters. Only then did he remember: it was a public holiday.

Still he walked on, past the moat of the Imperial Palace, until he reached the British embassy. He pressed the bell.

Nothing. Peering through the windows, all seemed empty and still. He made his way round to a side door for visa applications and rang the bell repeatedly. Just as he was turning to go he heard the door open behind him.

'Yes? And how can I help you?' The face was Japanese, a woman's, with the first crustiness of middle age. But the accent was English and almost absurdly pompous.

'I'm in a bit of trouble,' said Daniel. 'I need some advice and help.'

'I'm sorry but we are closed. It is a national holiday here in Japan.' She made it sound as if she had only just arrived in the country. 'I recommended you return tomorrow.'

'Isn't there somebody I could talk to?'

'I'm afraid not. Many people have gone away for the weekend to escape the horrid weather.'

'They can't all have gone.'

'I have told you, the embassy is closed. I would not be here except that I have some important typing to finish.'

'What about a telephone number – somebody who could help?'

'I am sorry,' she said firmly. 'I am not permitted to give you private numbers of staff.'

'But this is important. I'm in bad trouble. I haven't even got my passport. It's lost.'

She gave him a suspicious look. 'You *are* British?'

'Of course I'm British.'

'But I think you have no proof.'

'I haven't got a passport – that's one of the reasons I'm here. Now will you let me inside?'

She retreated, all but closing the door. 'I am sorry, but that is quite impossible.'

'It's urgent.' He took a step forward and she slammed the door shut.

'Will you let me inside?' he shouted. 'It's my embassy.'

'Only for real British,' he heard her voice, muffled through the door, then her footsteps retreating into the interior of the embassy.

He glared at the building. If he could find no help, then he would have to do the best to help himself. He made his way to the nearest station. Before long he was sitting on a train bound for Mount Takao.

He watched the familiar steep hills as they came into view through the window of the carriage. Their abrupt lines were softened into grey by the rain, like brackish ice-blocks in the first stages of melting.

Walking up from the station, he met the park official. The man seemed even more pleased to see him than he had been the previous time, shouting, 'Again! Again!'

They walked up towards the stalls and teashops. Daniel managed to explain that he had returned to resume his search. The man shook his had apologetically.

'No passport.'

Still Daniel gestured that he would climb and look.

'No – nothing.'

When Daniel repeated the gesture, the man nodded.

'Yes, I also.'

They began to follow the path. Above them, a storm was approaching and the rain was falling in an intense downpour.

The air began to chill as the waterfall came into sight. The priest was at work lighting candles. He looked up as they approached.

They reached the point where the path ran close alongside the ravine. Daniel lay down on the soaking ground and edged himself as far over the precipice as he could to peer down into the water. The light was poor – the downpour did not help – but he thought he saw a ledge.

Clambering up, he gestured into the gully. 'Down here.'

The official peered down. He nodded reluctantly and led the way up the hill to a point where the ravine was shallow enough to climb into.

The water of the stream, fresh from higher ground, was icy, while at several points the bottom was treacherously slippery. The current struggled over rocky cataracts which could only be crossed by crawling over the boulders.

Finally, up above the walls of the ravine, Daniel saw the avenue of trees that marked the spot where he had slipped. And by his feet there was a ledge, water pouring past just a few inches below. It was easily broad enough to catch a passport. But there was no passport.

The official gave a slow, sympathetic nod.

They began making their way out of the gully. On the surface once more, they systematically combed the area, scouring the land with dwindling enthusiasm, searching the litter bins, even the picnic area at the summit. Finally the official shook his head.

'No passport in my mountain.'

They walked slowly back down, Daniel wondering what he could do next. Sad and drenched as he was, he could think of nothing, not even where he might try and stay.

They reached the waterfall. The priest was still standing outside the temple, although his task of lighting the candles was complete. He called up to them. The park official gave Daniel a puzzled look.

'He wants to talk.'

They made their way down, removed their shoes, and were led inside the temple, to the main room. The priest was wearing glasses that gave him a strangely worldly appearance which contrasted markedly with the strong scent of incense hanging in the air, the crowd of religious statuettes, and the watery sounds penetrating from outside. He beckoned them to sit down.

With his hand he pointed out the path they had been following. He spoke a few brisk words to the official, who did his best to translate.

'He sees us looking.'

The priest turned to Daniel and indicated the waterfall. He stood up and began miming, slow and pious. With his hand he opened a gate and stepped gingerly into a substance that seemed to pull at his feet. He reached and stared up at a tall object, his eyes following its hurried downward movement.

With his fists he fought off what could have been tiny vicious birds fluttering around him. Then he relaxed and stepped into the object, his face calm and content. He sat down and closed his eyes. Then slowly opened them. He had found something lying in his lap. He plucked it up, opening and examining it.

He clapped his hands sharply and stood up, beckoning Daniel over to a nearby table. It was covered with figurines in a wealth of colours, sizes, and expressions, as well as brass jars containing flowers and offerings of fruit. And in the centre, half-concealed behind three oranges but propped respectfully against a rice bowl, was Daniel's battered British passport.

Daniel picked it up and eagerly thumbed through the pages. They were twisted and misshapen with damp, the handwritten entries were gone, but the photograph – his photograph – was intact.

He shook the priest's hand warmly. The man looked regretfully at the object, sad to lose so holy a possession.

Daniel and the park official walked back down to the

snack-bar. The official seemed as surprised and pleased as Daniel, shouting, 'Passport, passport.'

The snack-bar owner prepared a feast to celebrate – rice and sweet curry. He lit a paraffin heater on which Daniel dried the object as best he could. After they had eaten, the owner rummaged through his stock of souvenir and holiday goods and extracted a fountain pen. Daniel carefully rewrote all the details that the water had dissolved.

He thanked them both and made his way back towards the station. For the first time in quite a while, he felt in some control of his future.

His next step was simple – money. He decided to make a last attempt to corner and confront Mrs Chiba.

Chapter Nine

Daniel strode out of Zudanuma station and looked up at the window of the school. This time there was a marked sign of activity. The glass was grey with condensation.

From the bottom of the stairway he could hear the hum of voices floating down. The door was half-open. Through it he saw Mrs Kamakura, not behind her desk but standing, in her hand a glass of fizzy liquid. She caught sight of him and stared with deep puzzlement. It was no stage reaction.

The walls inside were hung with balloons and garish paper decorations. And the cramped rooms of the school were filled with people. All of Daniel's students seemed to be present, talking and drinking.

Near the door stood a westerner Daniel had never met before, with a thick red beard and a face that glowed with sincerity. 'You're not Daniel Thayne are you?' His accent was Canadian. 'But that's great – I can get some notes on what the classes have done so far.'

'You're a new teacher?'

'Of course.' The Canadian seemed puzzled that he did not know. 'So how did you make it? I heard you'd already gone.'

'Gone where?'

The Canadian was unsure if the reply was a joke. 'Back home, of course.'

'Why should I go anywhere?'

An uneasy laugh. 'Yuh — I guess so.'

Students were clustering around Daniel, excited by his unexpected appearance.

'You are here,' exclaimed one of them, an old spinster. 'Mrs Chiba say you are already leave Japan.'

'Did she?'

The same puzzled look. 'Your father — he is recover?'

'What did Mrs Chiba say?'

'She say he is very ill. I am so sorry.'

Others were voicing their sympathy, their happiness that they would be able to say goodbye.

'All students want to see you before you go,' said the old maid. 'Only this morning I receive letter saying I must come to party for your goodbye. Only this morning, but I know I must come — I left office early time to come. We are all arrive. Then Mrs Chiba tells that your father is more ill and you must go before — so sad. But now you are here.'

'I certainly am.' He saw Mrs Chiba's head bobbing excitedly in the distance, in a circle of office ladies. He pushed his way through to her.

'I managed to come after all.'

She stared at him, eyes even wider than usual. Conscious of the students all around, she did her best to recover herself. Daniel watched with a certain pleasure her attempts to look relaxed and pleased.

'We are so happy you can come,' she said at last.

'Are you? It was quite a surprise for me to find you'd laid on this party for my farewell.'

She stole a quick look at the office ladies. She need not have worried. None had reached even the intermediary standard in their English. Their nods and smiles showed no enlightenment.

'We must have happy goodbye for you.'

'Must you? And how is my father?'

'Your father?' she said awkwardly. 'We all hope he is well. We are so sad for him.'

The brows of the office ladies furrowed in concern.

'I don't think you need worry too much,' began Daniel. 'When I spoke with him, just the other day . . .'

'Danieru, please,' broke in Mrs Chiba. 'I must private talk with you – special private matters.'

'And what might they be?'

'Good for you – very special.'

He frowned. 'They'd better be.'

She led the way through the throng, Daniel waving away request after request for news of his father. Out onto the landing beyond the school entrance. He pushed the door shut behind them, abruptly sealing in the din of the party.

'Now, what is all this?'

She drew in her breath, gathering strength for her reply. 'Danieru, you want students to think good things of you?'

'Of course.'

'That is what I decide. So I make party for you to leave Japan and Vital School.'

'Fine. Except that I haven't left either.'

She shook her head disapprovingly. 'Danieru – my husband knows about you. Me also. We decide it is better that student do not remember you as bad teacher who betray your school.'

'Betray?'

She looked at him solemnly. 'I am not such stupid person. I notice when again and again you are busy that you cannot teach private lesson. And you want all money but will not tell why. And you will not say good things of student to make them stay at Vital. Then my husband sees you talking with Australian man who works for Happiness School. So I understand.'

'You think I'm working for Happiness?'

'Of course. But still I decide that it is better to have happy goodbye for students' good memories. I do not tell them how you betray them. I say you must leave Japan because your father is ill.'

'Come off it Mrs Chiba – this has nothing to do with students' good memories. You were worried that I was going to leave Vital and take all my students with me to Happiness. And why shouldn't I, since you never pay me?'

She gave out a snort. 'We do not know what you may do. We are so sad that you do not show good respect and honour for your employer. We are disappointed.'

'Is that so? And you decide to find another teacher and even hold my farewell party, all without telling me. I'm afraid I'm also rather disappointed.'

She shook her head dismissively. 'For the school we must do.'

'You must? Well, I'd better tell you what I must do. For the good of the students I must go back in there,' he indicated the door of the school, 'and tell them that my father is not ill. I must explain that you have been lying – not just to me, but to all of them – and finally I must recommend they join a school with a more honest manager, such as Happiness.'

'You would not. Students will think badly of you that you betray school.'

'Perhaps. But they'd think more badly of you for lying to them.'

'They will not believe you – you are only teacher. I control school.'

Daniel pulled the door ajar, releasing a buzz of voices. 'You're sure they'll believe you rather than me?'

She pushed it shut. 'This is mad wrong. We must not

fight – we work together in same company. Better that we talk.'

'Fine – let's talk. I'll begin by stating what I feel I'm owed. There are all the wages that I should have been paid. And there's a ticket to Hong Kong – that can be for all the tricks you've tried to play on me.'

She shook her head gravely. 'Such bad attitude. Ticket maybe we can give, but money is impossible – impossible for school.'

'That's a great pity.' He pulled open the door, letting out the full din of the party. She clutched his arm.

'Wait. Maybe school can afford some money – little.'

'All of it – or I tell the students to join Happiness.'

She glared at him. 'I think you are bad man. You have no heart, no loyalty to company.'

'And?'

'My husband will collect money that you love so much. And ticket to go away to foreign country. We will be please that you are go.'

'I need them this evening.'

'He can get these at airport. He will give them after party is finish.'

'No – before then.'

'Impossible – maybe you will take them and make bad talk anyway.'

'All right – show them to me during the party and hand them over after it ends.'

She gave a reluctant nod of her head. 'But you must good farewell to students.'

'A farewell?'

'Of course. We will say your father is more better. And at end students will form long line for happy goodbye. You will shake hands with all men and kiss women on their cheek.' She pointed to her own. 'Here.'

Daniel shrugged his shoulders. 'All right.' He walked back into the school, where he was quickly surrounded by students.

'Your father is better?'

'You will come back to Japan?'

Out of the corner of his eye he saw Mrs Chiba whisper to her husband, who then padded inconspicuously out of the door.

'You like Japan?'

Mrs Chiba climbed onto the seat of a chair and barked a demand for silence. She explained, first in English and then in Japanese, how Daniel's father was still ill but had recovered enough for Daniel to delay his departure by a few hours. He had done this because he had wanted so much to say goodbye to his students. She began clapping, quickly joined by those listening.

'You are sad for your father?'

'You will come back to Japan?'

Daniel found it hard to concentrate on the questions he was asked, he was so excited by the thought that he would shortly be away from the whole country, from the Chibas and Haradas and all the scheming and intrigue that went with them.

He did not have to talk for long. He was soon relieved by an intense bout of photograph-taking. Most of the students had brought cameras, all of a similar kind: a compact, foolproof device with a built-in flash. The classrooms were soon rebounding with regular explosions of light.

The photograph-taking was a lengthy process. First there were the group poses, of different classes. Each had to be taken again and again as individuals left the group to take their personal photograph, then handed the camera to another and hurried back for a pose that included themselves. Daniel, of course, had to be in all of them.

Even when these were finally over, the flashes continued – now for informal, candid shots. By this point the beer was beginning to have its effect and a change of mood was becoming apparent.

The giggles of the schoolgirls were growing louder and more shrill. Singing was breaking out amongst the men – three in particular had made off to one of the classrooms with a huge can of beer. Soon a nasty yelping filtered back through the plastic partitions.

Among the office ladies, sentimentality was rife. 'You will come back to Japan?' They asked the question again and again, with a real concern for his welfare. In their eyes he was leaving Japan for a dangerous and disorganized place: the rest of the world. He might never come back.

And the crying began. It started small, with a solitary schoolgirl standing in a corner, snivelling behind her thick glasses. But it quickly spread through the other schoolgirls. Then to Izumi, her stockings already collected despairingly around her ankles. She wept profusely, as if forgiving Daniel his failings in her education.

Soon the office ladies had joined her, and the old maids. Finally even the housewives succumbed – sensible Noriko, Kyoko, then fashionable Chizuru, dabbing her face with a tissue to prevent her make-up from being spoiled.

'You will come back to Japan?' The question had turned to pleading, for his own good.

Daniel stood, aware of the noise all around him. The singing and giggling and crying and constant questions. It was with some relief that he saw Mr Chiba pad in through the doorway.

He made his way through the confusion towards him, as did Mrs Chiba. The three of them retreated to the quiet of the landing outside, where Mr Chiba extracted from his pocket a thick envelope.

'Here it is,' baked his wife. 'That you want so much that you threaten your employer.'

It was all there. Daniel felt a particular triumph at the sight of the flight ticket to Hong Kong booked for the afternoon of the following day, his name written clearly across it.

Mrs Chiba snatched it away. 'Not now. After party.'

They returned to the uproar. Mrs Chiba clambered onto a chair for the final announcement. Despite the power of her voice, it was some moments before she was able to quell the noise all around her.

'Now please. The goodbye ceremony.'

She directed the students into a long queue, pointing towards the door, where Daniel stood.

The noise quickly subsided, but the emotion did not. The crying and singing gave way to silent weeping and downward glances. The men stared ahead of them, as solemn as if they were attending a funeral.

The ceremony began. Murmurings of 'Goodbye, goodbye,' repeated with hypnotic regularity. Daniel did not know how to react to the outburst of grief. It was not as if he had ever felt himself to be particularly popular amongst his students, let alone a conscientious teacher. His lessons had been accepted largely because so few of his students were genuinely interested in learning English.

The faces passed by in front of him. Mostly unattractive women – bad teeth, overplump faces, sad eyes that were red from crying. He found himself looking down away from them, made awkward by the whole occasion.

Shaking of hands, kisses on cheeks, murmurings of 'Goodbye, goodbye'. The procession was finally reaching its end. Daniel was dimly aware of Mrs Chiba next to him, whispering agitatedly to her husband.

The last in the parade. Still looking down, Daniel saw the grey of a jacket and proffered his hand. It was gripped rather than shaken, as if the man had no intention of letting go. Looking up, Daniel found himself staring into the face of Mr Harada. He heard the door close behind him.

'Who is he?' clucked Mrs Chiba angrily. 'He is not student. He is not pay for party.'

Daniel twisted his hand free and turned to the door. The way was blocked by Toshihiko and Masayuki. The squat elder brother gave him a sharp shove that propelled him back into the room.

Mrs Chiba stopped clucking. Her husband stepped back, raising his hand to shield his face, although nobody had offered him any threat.

Mr Harada shouted a few brief words to Mrs Chiba. Daniel understood their meaning well enough from the look of alarm that passed across her face. Toshihiko opened the door. She needed no further prompting, scrambling out, her husband after her. The door was closed again.

'What the hell are you doing here?' demanded Daniel.

Mr Harada raised his hand to quiet him. 'You must not shout – it is not good. Already I am surprise that you behave so wrongly – that you lie to me.'

'Me? But it's you who's been lying.'

Mr Harada's voice became very quiet. 'I think you must be careful what you say.' From his pocket he took a card. 'This afternoon I go to my daughter's house, to search for you if you are hurt. I am worry for you. And I find this.'

The card's message was written in English and Japanese, all in the unmistakable angular handwriting of Mrs Chiba.

VERY SAD

Our teacher Daniel must leave Japan because his father is become so old and sick. Such pity. But on Friday we have lovely party to say goodbye and also for English speak experience. Please Y1500. Beer and snack – all free.

CALL MY TELEPHONE. YES!

'I was surprised,' said Mr Harada drily. 'All these days my family work hard to make good house for you and Keiko. All this time you say you want to marry Keiko. But secretly you tell this school that you will leave Japan – they make this party for you.'

'I didn't know anything about this party,' protested Daniel. 'The Chibas organized the whole thing without letting me know – they wanted to sack me without my finding out.'

'You did not know of this party. But you came.'

'That was pure chance – I came here to speak with them about quite another matter.'

'Another matter?' Mr Harada pondered. 'Interesting.'

'Since when do I have to account for myself to you,' said Daniel, suddenly angry – the more he tried to defend himself the worse his position seemed to become. 'It's you who should be giving an explanation to me. Why did you tell me Keiko was pregnant?'

'She is pregnant – with your child.'

'She's not – I've seen that she's not.'

'No,' said Mr Harada quietly. 'Even now you are lie, like all foreigner.' There was no doubt of indecision in the man's face. Daniel realized that Keiko could have been lying to him too.

'But I can prove she's not,' he said. 'Just take her to a clinic.'

'There is no need.'

'Then just ask her – you'll see.'

'I question her if I believe you, and I do not believe you – your behaviour is too wrong. You say you will marry, then you go away. You must learn truth.'

'But this is mad,' burst out Daniel. 'It's all mad.'

Mr Harada shook his head. 'You are wrong seeing. We must talk that you see correctly. Not here – school is not place for talk. We will go to better place.'

'I'm not going anywhere,' said Daniel firmly.

'It is better that you come.'

'You have no rights over me – I'll do what I like.'

'And what do you like?'

'Right now I want to go for a farewell drink with some of my students. I told them to wait downstairs.'

Mr Harada gave a shake of his head, so slight as to be almost imperceptible. 'They do not.'

'Think what you like.' Daniel turned to the door. Masayuki pushed him suddenly off balance. Toshihiko looked on with approval, satisfied that his own shame and punishment were being avenged.

'I'd recommend that you let me go freely now,' said Daniel. 'Otherwise it could lead to trouble with the law.'

'You have no law,' said Mr Harada briefly.

'I can call some.' Daniel filled his lungs and let out a great yell.

Mr Harada gave him a slow stare. 'You must not shout,' he advised. 'It is bad.'

Daniel drew in breath for a second roar, but did not get so far as making the sound. At a signal from his father, Masayuki lumbered forwards towards him, drew back his arm, and delivered a swift blow to Daniel's stomach. Almost at the same instant, Daniel felt a sharp pain at the back of his neck. He found it hard to breathe. The room around him blurred into sickly greys and flipped upside down.

Chapter Ten

Daniel came to in the car as it drew to a halt. Colours still blurred into greys. The pavement seemed to tilt alarmingly as he was bundled out of the car door.

'Up here,' said Mr Harada. Daniel was half pushed, half carried up a stairway. At the top was what appeared to be a hotel foyer: a desk with row upon row of keys dancing on hooks behind it. The walls seemed to be swimming, but swirled slowly enough for him to notice their oddly old-fashioned colour – a dark Victorian scarlet – and the electric lights that had been made to look like gaslamps.

There were people everywhere. In the distance, darting to the desk to take a key, was Mr Toshio with his thick mask-like skin. Women lounged on chairs, leant against the walls – some huge, some small and dark.

Daniel found himself propped up against a wall. A fleshy face leered in front of his own. With it came a familiar odour – sour, sweaty. The lips opened.

'You come back, Englishman.'

He recognized the overdone make-up below her eyes – purple and black.

'You come back for Japanese girl?' A squawk of laughter. 'And how is your girlfriend?'

Somewhere else Mr Harada's voice barked a command and the face pulled out from view. Daniel found himself propelled along a corridor, then through a doorway into a small room. The door slammed shut behind him and the lock clicked to.

Staggering, he saw a bed, sheets rumpled. He tumbled across it, feeling the sheets still warm. And he lay there, his vision gradually became clearer, lines more distinct. He wondered if he was concussed. He wondered what the symptoms of concussion might be.

He began to recover, observing more about the room. Its function was clear from its contents: no windows, a solitary bed, just large enough for its purpose, and a clinical sink built into the wall, for washing afterwards. The only decoration was a small framed photograph of a western girl baring her thighs.

Not much time had elapsed since it had last been used. A cocktail of odours still hung in the air, while amongst the sheets he discovered a large yellow stain, damp and visibly still growing. He shifted away, so as not to touch it.

Outside one voice was discernible amongst the babble: Mr Harada, speaking slowly and monotonously. Daniel guessed he was using the telephone.

He lay back against the wall. He wished he had not passed out, then he would know where he was. But at least he finally knew what he was dealing with. He knew about the Haradas' 'company' and had seen part of it at first hand.

And he could guess how the man with the squint knew of the family. The small dark-skinned girls he had seen had been Filipino women, the other main group of work-permit regulation dodgers besides western English teachers. The man with the squint must have worked for the Immigration Department, just as he had claimed, and had been sent to check if the Haradas had any illegal employees. Realizing that Daniel was entangled with them, he had decided to warn him. Judging by the nervousness of his warning, Daniel guessed that the Haradas had gained a strong hold over the man.

A family of pimps – that was what he was up against. The discovery made Mr Harada's attitude over his daughter all the more bizarre. Daniel doubted that to point this out would help him.

As his senses sharpened, his injuries made themselves more acutely felt. He remembered with jarring clarity his ill-treatment at the hands of the two brothers.

He sat up. He needed something with which to defend himself – anything. He examined the bed, seeking some part he could detach, but instead of legs there were welded metal rails. He thought of the sink – he could throw it – but found it was well secured to the wall. Finally he took down the framed photograph. The covering was plastic, not glass as he had hoped.

Then he lifted up the mattress of the bed. Beneath he found a leather whip with a stubby wooden handle. He slipped it into place behind the belt of his trousers.

Shouting outside – Mr Harada giving orders. Then the click of the key in the lock and the door swung open. Masayuki and his father stood over Daniel.

'You are better?' asked Mr Harada.

'A little.'

'Good. Now we can talk.' He sat down on the bed beside Daniel. 'I do not understand you,' he said thoughtfully. 'You want me to hate you? You want me to be angry?'

Daniel remained silent. If he had learnt anything from his encounters with the family, it was that the less he said the better.

'I know foreigners,' the man resumed. 'Always they are break things – break marriage, break life, break truth. I know them well.'

He gave Daniel a careful look. 'But when I first meet with you I see from your face that you are not only bad. Like all foreigner your behave is wrong – you take girl for play, you have no plan. But I decide maybe you can become better – with help – and become warmer heart.

'I want to help you. Then you lie, you run away. You make me too angry.'

He let out a slight sigh. 'Even now I wonder: can you become better man?'

There was something in the way he spoke, a preaching tone, like a missionary set on conversion. It reminded Daniel of somebody. He realized that Mr Harada had the same thought as the students at the party: a determination that he should not be surrendered to the rest of the world, a lost soul. But in Mr Harada's voice there was also an underlying threat.

'My daughter is forgive you,' he resumed. 'Still she does not hate you, despite all that you do against her. Still she wants to help you in Japan.'

Daniel broke his silence. 'You want things to go on as before?' he asked cautiously. 'Go on as if nothing had happened?'

'Maybe. If I believe your behave will be correct; that you will not lie.' He looked thoughtfully round the room. 'Hotel is still ready for wedding party, for tomorrow. And Mr Toshio kindly say he can arrange work for you teaching in company.'

'The company? You mean here?'

'Not this building. Company is large – many place.'

Daniel's bafflement got the better of him. 'I just don't understand,' he said slowly. 'You're so concerned for Keiko's honour; that she should be respectably married. And yet you run this place. What of the honour of the women here?'

Mr Harada glared wearily at him, as if depressed by the ignorance his question betrayed. 'They are different. They are company, not family.'

'I see.'

A pause. Daniel heard some commotion outside – some clients had arrived and were being hustled into rooms with the women they had chosen. Doors slammed shut.

'And if I say no to all this?' asked Daniel. 'What then?'

'It is better you do not say.' Mr Harada spoke quietly. This made his words far more menacing than if he had shouted threats. 'Better for you.'

Silence. Daniel tried to think. He could not bring himself to agree to the demand. But he was too frightened to voice an outright refusal.

'Well?'

'I just don't know,' he said at last. 'I need time to consider. It's so important. I need to be alone for a while, to work it all out. Somewhere quiet, away from here.'

Mr Harada scrutinized him. 'There is little time. Wedding is for tomorrow.'

'A few hours – just enough time to think.'

Mr Harada pondered for a moment, then said, 'My sons will take you to family house – you will be enough quiet there. I will come in two hours, when I have finish business here. By then you must decide.'

He signalled to Masayuki, who pulled open the bedroom door. Daniel clambered to his feet. All he had done was win a slight delay. He was aware that in two hours' time he would be no readier to reach a decision than he was now. He always seemed to be seeking delays rather than solutions.

He stepped out into the corridor. The women idling all around glanced at him with curiosity. The chief whore squeezed her face into a smile and stuck out her tongue.

Toshihiko came towards him. 'You come back now,' he observed, as if Daniel had been abroad.

'Maybe.'

'You must not go away – you make big trouble for us and you.'

They walked towards the exit. Toshihiko stayed close at Daniel's side, while Masayuki marched on just a few yards ahead, glancing back to check all was well.

'Two hours,' called out their father from behind them.

Past the reception desk, Mr Toshio dully watching them. And they reached the top of the stairway. It was then that Daniel heard a yell reverberating from below. For a moment he wondered if it was some victim of the Haradas.

'Who's that?' he asked.

'I think customer.'

They had just begun descending the stairway when Daniel heard another shout. This one needed no explaining – the voice was familiar.

'Naaaww,' it went. 'I tell ya mate, this is a great place – great girls. You'll love it.'

'I am not so sure,' replied a timid voice, Japanese. 'It is all right?'

' 'Course it is.'

Now it was Toshihiko's turn to be worried. He took a sharp grip on Daniel's arm. 'Your friend?'

'Doesn't sound like any friend of mine.'

'That is good.'

The first voice yelled again, then let out a burble of Japanese, the same phrase repeated drunkenly again and again.

'Turn it down will you,' demanded the Australian. 'You'll frighten off the tarts.'

By now Daniel and Toshihiko were already halfway

down the stairway, with Masayuki some yards ahead of them. There was a clatter and into view below them rolled Jake and two Japanese in suits, ties askew, one supporting the other as he staggered inside. Jake glanced up.

'Hey – Brit. Whad'ya doing here?'

'So he is your friend.' Toshihiko's grip on Daniel's arm tightened, but not enough. Daniel used all his weight and strength to twist him ahead and propel him forward down the stairs, where he collided nastily with Masayuki, himself just turning round. Daniel had barely enough time to reach beneath his jacket. Masayuki pushed his brother out of the way and lumbered up towards him, only to be struck on the jaw with the wooden handle of the whip. His bulk reeled. He toppled, bringing down his brother, and both crashed back down.

'Wahssup?' demanded Jake.

'Run,' shouted Daniel, springing down, three steps at a time.

Jake's reactions were quick. He did not pause to question the situation. He bolted.

Daniel had the momentum of his downward flight. He was able to force his way over and through the two brothers now at the bottom of the stairway, scrambling to get up.

Past the baffled office-workers. Out of the building, into the welcoming rain. A glimpse of the hurtling figure of Jake, already some distance away. Daniel ran after him. Jake should know which way to go.

On through narrow streets. Daniel saw the turreted façade of the love hotel. He was in Zudanuma, in the red-light district just behind Vital School.

Jake darted round corner after corner, until they were in near darkness, footsteps clapping noisily into the void. Jake stole a glance over his shoulder, then slowed to a halt.

They stood, gasping for breath. Jake was the first to overcome his panting. 'It was only you – I thought it was one of them after me.'

'No.'

'So what was all that about?'

'Keiko's family – they turned nasty.'

'So I noticed. What the hell were you all doing in there?'

'That's where they took me – they run the place.'

Jake's eyes narrowed. 'They run that joint?'

'Yes – I think they have several.'

Jake glanced down the streets around them. 'Shit. That's all I need. And they saw my face – I'm sure of it.'

'I'm in trouble.'

'You bet you are.'

'Look, you know this country better than I do – I need your help.'

'Sure you do – and if I give it I'll get caught up in all your shit.'

'You could get me out of this – I know it.'

'Sorry Brit – not my mess.'

'At least give me some idea of what to do.'

'I couldn't say.'

'Why won't you help?'

'Told you – it's not my problem.'

'You frightened or something?' said Daniel angrily.

'I'll tell you this much,' said the Australian slowly. 'If I was in your shoes I'd be shit scared.'

For a moment Daniel wondered if he should try and reach the Chibas' house. But the Haradas might be waiting – it would be an absurd risk.

He began walking, following the street down which Jake had gone. It was one of constant twists and junctions, and he had soon lost all sense of direction. Down a side street he saw an opening of stronger light. He stole towards it. A clatter of footsteps sent him hurrying into the shadow. Peering out, he saw three businessmen, arms on each other's shoulders, walking precariously forward. He stepped out towards them.

'D'you speak English?'

The three halted, teetering dangerously. One laughed. 'America,' he called out. 'You like drink America?'

'Not now. I need your help. D'you know where I can find . . .'

'Drink drink – whisky beer whisky. We go drink now America?'

'I don't need a drink – I need your help.'

'Whisky is good. America whisky.'

'All right, forget it.' He turned and hurried on, pursued by shouts.

'America – where you go America?'

He reached the light – a shopping street, now shuttered and silent. He stepped cautiously forwards, then suddenly halted. In the distance he saw a flash of headlamps. He stood quite still, watching. The glare grew brighter, then, where the road curved almost out of view, he glimpsed black metalwork. And it was gone.

He pressed on. The shopping street curved to the left. He kept to the right so as to see ahead as far as possible. Until he caught sight of exactly what he had been hoping to find – a police box, light shining out. Within was visible a figure in uniform, slumped at his desk, sitting out his night duty.

Daniel pushed open the door to the sanctuary, startling its inhabitant.

'You speak English?'

The man shook his head.

'As if it matters. You can see I need help.' He pointed back through the open doorway. 'Bad people outside – following me.' He clenched his fist and struck the air in a swift fighting movement.

The policeman frowned in confusion. He motioned Daniel to sit down.

'But don't you see – it's urgent. Call somebody who can speak English.'

The policeman looked at him, not understanding. Daniel picked up the telephone from his desk.

'Call somebody with English – *Eigo*.'

The man pointed to his watch – it was two-thirty – and shook his head. He gestured Daniel to sit down.

'But this is important.'

The man gestured again, angry now. With reluctance Daniel obeyed, in the hope that by doing so he would increase the man's concern. But he only asked for Daniel's passport, then thumbed disapprovingly through the parchment-like pages. Finally he took from a drawer a white form, several pages long, all of it in Japanese. He proffered a ballpoint and pointed to the first space.

'*Namae, namae.*'

'But this is ridiculous – there's no time to start filling in forms.'

'*Namae, namae.*'

'All right – if it'll get you to take some action.' Impatiently Daniel scribbled his name in the first space. The policeman pointed to the next.

'Addlessu.'

He wrote that out too. The next space was for his telephone number. After that came a more puzzling demand – from the man's miming Daniel guessed that it was either for his date of birth or his father's Christian name.

It was then that he saw them: headlamps illuminating the street.

He pointed towards the glare. 'They're out there – bad people.' He mimed turning a steering wheel. The policeman stared at him, annoyed at the interruption to their progress on the fifth section of the form.

Daniel tried to imagine if the Haradas would respect the sanctity of the police box. It did not seem very likely. He looked at the policeman, trying to size him up as an ally. He was burly enough, but there was something in the way he sat so still and unconcerned, frowning at the form on the desk between them.

The headlamps grew brighter outside. Daniel jumped to his feet and ran, pursued by a cry of astonished rebuke.

He left the main road, down a side street. Then twisted into an even smaller side street, but found it was a cul-de-sac. At the end he discovered a narrow alley.

It was dark and half-filled with rubbish bags. Edging his way along it he saw that it led straight back towards the police box. He could see the policeman, still staring out in the direction he had first run.

It was not a place where Daniel wanted to linger – the alley was too narrow and awkward for any movement, while it would be easy to cut him off. But with the Haradas' car drawing steadily nearer he had no thoughts of making a break for it.

The road in front of the police box lit up – the car was approaching from a quite unexpected direction.

It stopped just at the end of the alley. For a moment Daniel almost panicked, imagining they had somehow guessed his hiding place. But Mr Harada and his two sons did not glance towards him. They crossed to the police box.

Daniel was just able to see over the top of the car. The

policeman shook Mr Harada's hand, as if he knew him. The sound of their conversation drifted back. Mr Harada seemed to be asking all the questions. Then the policeman held up a white form. Mr Harada examined it, nodding. The policeman pointed out the way Daniel had run.

The Haradas climbed back into their car. The vehicle drew slowly away.

Across the road Daniel could see the policeman busy at the telephone, making call after call, each with careful reference to the white form.

He waited until the car engine was quite out of earshot before creeping back down the alleyway, eager to be as far from the police box as possible.

He began walking through the darkened streets. All that mattered now was to leave the district, escape beyond the range of the Haradas' searches and last out the night somewhere.

In the distance he glimpsed the floodlit insignia cube of a department store; he felt it was familiar but was not sure. He tried to plot a course across the landscape, but was quickly baffled by the winding roads.

Ahead he saw another brightly illuminated street. Glancing down it he faintly recognized some of the buildings. Neon signs − unlit. It was only when he was walking down it that he saw, looming out of the darkness, the Disney-style façade of a love hotel.

Now he knew where he was − exactly where he did not want to be.

He turned to retrace his steps down the side road, only to hear in the distance the patter of light footsteps. In another direction he thought he saw the flash of those same headlights.

He did not wait to discover if the dangers were of any substance − his nerves were too frayed for that. His whole being cried out for cover, for somewhere to hide. And a few yards away he saw a stairway leading down into the ground, beneath a concrete block. It would do.

The steps were deep and uneven. He touched the walls to help keep balance; they were clammy in the warm damp. A sign glowed feebly above the doorway at the bottom: 'Don Up Bar 11P.M.–4.30A.M.

He paused, unsure. But was decided by the tap of footsteps echoing down to him. He pushed open the door.

His eyes focused. Half standing, half leaning against a table, he saw what he at first imagined to be a woman. Fishnet stockings, daintily pointed shoes, short tight dress and a blouse that hung limply over a flat, pigeon-chested torso. Daubed with lip gloss and heavy white make-up, the face was a touch too square. The hair was in the short, cropped style of a company worker.

There was an awkward silence. The figure glanced at Daniel with curiosity. Daniel looked round the room, a plain-walled bar, empty and ordinary enough except for its solitary inhabitant. From another room came the rhythmic thumping of disco music. Daniel had never seen such a place. He wondered if it too was run by the Haradas. He just had to hope not.

The white-painted face at last broke the silence. 'Yes?'

'Well – d'you have any beer?'

'Difficult.' The white face tilted and let out a giggle. 'You are not usual customer.'

'Does that matter? All I want is a beer.'

'Only?'

'That's right – only beer.'

The face poured disappointedly. 'Yes yes – all right. Sit down.'

Daniel sat at one of the tables. The door to the disco was ajar and he caught a momentary glimpse of two figures swirling past, ballroom style.

'Beer for you.' The face leant over Daniel's shoulder to place a bottle and glass before him. 'America?'

'England.'

'So nice.' He danced away to the entrance, where he resumed his pose propped against the table.

Daniel sipped his beer. If he could only stay for an hour or so the Haradas would surely begin searching somewhere else. He would be safe.

The doorway to the disco flashed with changing colours: red then green then blue then red. The words of the song were just discernible over the dull beat: 'Gotta get up, get up. Gotta get down, get down. Ride the funk on funky alley.'

'You live London?' called out the white face.

'Yes, London,' replied Daniel.

'So nice.'

The two figures spun momentarily into view through the half-open door. One was similar to the white-painted face in costume, girth and haircut – Daniel guessed he also worked there. The other, who had his back to Daniel, was plumper. There was something familiar about him.

The white face had observed Daniel's interest. He dropped down from the table. 'You like disco?'

'Not much.'

'You like dance?'

'Afraid not.'

'Then what you like?'

Daniel got up from the table. 'Maybe I like to watch.'

The white face gave him a look of mock disapproval. 'Watch? So bad.'

Daniel neared the door of the disco. The words rang

out louder. 'Gotta get down, get down. Ride the funk on funky alley.'

He felt a slight jab in the arm, from a pointed fingernail. 'I think you like to dance.'

'Sorry.'

'So bad, so bad.'

Daniel pushed the door fully open. The room seemed to change in size and shape with each new flash of the coloured lights. As they changed from green to blue, he caught a clear view of the two in their spinning embrace. Daniel recognized the clothes of the plumper figure, the brown slacks and polo-neck shirt. The flashing bulbs illuminated the soft features of Mr Chiba.

They turned and he saw Daniel standing in the doorway, watching him. For an instant he froze, before lurching back into motion, as if in the wild hope that his anonymity had not been lost.

'Mr Chiba,' called out Daniel, in a voice loud enough to overcome the thump of the music. 'And how are you?'

'Your friend?' asked the white face, in a puzzled voice. 'You do not say.'

Mr Chiba slowly separated himself from his partner and walked across to the doorway. 'Why do you come here?' he demanded, his voice full with brittle anger. 'This is private place – not for you.'

'I just dropped in. I was looking forward to having another talk with you.'

'Private bar – you must leave this place.' He shouted a demand to the white face, but baffled and alarmed by the dispute, the man showed no signs of intervention.

'I'll be happy to go,' said Daniel, 'once we've settled our agreement.'

'No – impossible,' cried Mr Chiba, his anger already

beginning to show cracks. 'My wife says you have break agreement by invite bad people to school.'

'I see. And what does she say about you coming to this place?'

'Not important.'

'You're sure?'

Mr Chiba's anger deserted him. He stared at Daniel, suddenly quiet. 'But I cannot give these things to you. What do I say to her?'

'Tell her you've lost them, or that they were stolen. Tell her what you like.'

'But she will think . . .'

'Perhaps she will. But isn't that better than her knowing?'

Mr Chiba bowed his head. 'Possible.'

'No question – it's better.'

Mr Chiba let out a spluttering cough. ' She is such hard woman to live with. Always shout, always angry. Very big voice.'

'Why did you marry her?'

'Meeting was arrange by marriage woman – match-maker. Hard to say no. And before marry she is more quiet, not so big voice. But now sometimes I like go away from her to this place, for holiday time.'

'I see.'

Mr Chiba uttered a few words to the white face, then followed him back to the reception area. His jacket was hanging on a rail. From the pocket he took the thick envelope, trotting back to proffer the object to Daniel.

'You will not tell her?'

'No – don't worry.'

'You must understand – she is difficult woman to live with.'

'I can imagine.'

He gave the envelope to Daniel. Holding it tight in his hand, Daniel made his way out of the bar and cautiously ascended the stairway, listening as he went. All was silent; the street was quite deserted. He looked round at the drab buildings and they seemed to blur and become indistinct; like the faces he had seen on the airport train, he felt as if he was no longer quite in the country.

He made his way through the back streets, cautiously approaching the station. There would be no trains to the airport before morning – he had some time to kill. He decided to go back to his apartment and check for any signs of life. With luck the Haradas would be too busy searching for him in Zudanuma to keep watch in Takasago – he would be able to retrieve his slides and cameras.

The station loomed up ahead, filling the open horizon of the backstreet. Daniel picked his way forward, watching. A couple of late-night drunks staggered into view. And in front of the station, as he hoped, was a taxi.

Through the windows he watched the landscape flitting by. No rain, only columns of steam rising from the open sewers. He directed the driver to Takasago station. Safer to walk the last part.

Past the darkened shops to the crossing. Ahead he saw the children's school – as silent as a ruin – and his own apartment. No light shone through the windows.

He moved more easily, already planning what he should take besides the slides and cameras, what he might need. It was when he was beneath the building, stepping quietly towards the entrance stairway, that he heard the sound.

'Shhhhhhh.'

He glanced round. Nothing. He wondered for a moment if it could be caused by the sewers.

'Shhhhhhh.'

This time he was more ready – he was able to catch the direction of the noise. Some yards away, in a shadow, he made out the darker outline of a short figure. As he crept cautiously forwards, it stepped into the light. It was Keiko.

He stared about him for any others. There were none. 'What are you . . .'

'Shhhhhh,' she silenced him. 'I wait for you all night,' she whispered. 'For warning.'

'What warning?'

She pointed up to the apartment. 'They wait for you – my uncles. They wait in the dark.'

'But how did you know I'd come here?'

'You like camera and photography too much – I know that of you. So I come, for warning to show my sorriness to you.'

Daniel was unsure. She had lied so much before. Who was to say if there really was anybody in his apartment. She might be trying to slow him down, delay him so that when he returned her family could be ready.

'I'm going to have a look.'

'You must not.'

'Too bad.' He began making his way up to the stairway, as silently as he could. Reaching the level of the windows he paused and peered inside; it was too dark to see anything.

He waited, listening. Nothing. Then a throaty cough, thick and sleep ridden. He picked his way down the stairway as quickly as he could without giving himself away.

'Now you believe?' demanded Keiko, a little crossly.

'I suppose so.'

'We must go from here – not safe. We go to love hotel.'

'What love hotel?'

'I know near here one that is good for us.'

The more she tried to suggest, the more suspicious he became. He was not even sure of her claim that it had been her uncles in the apartment. He had heard a cough but no more. It was possible that somebody might be trying to help him, perhaps the man with the squint or some observant neighbour.

But he did not dare go back up the stairway. He would have to wait somewhere till morning – try then. He glanced at Keiko. To leave her might be more dangerous than taking her with him. She could contact her parents and tell them of his whereabouts.

'All right – but I'll pick the hotel.'

There were no taxis anywhere. They walked for some distance, Keiko keeping always a little behind Daniel, until they reached a main road. Before long they found a love hotel, with the façade not of a castle but of an ocean liner.

Daniel booked the room, asking for one without a telephone. He locked the door as soon as they were inside. Keiko sat on the edge of the circular bed that dominated the room. A panel of intricate switches controlled the revolving mechanism.

She turned to him. 'I know you still hate me that I make such bad things to you.'

He crossed to the porthole-shaped window behind her. Reaching up, he concealed the door key on the curtain rail. 'I don't hate you.'

'It is true?' She seemed a little placated. 'But my father say you go soon from Japan.'

'Yes.'

She gave a quick nod of her head. 'Of course. You must.' Standing up, she stepped across to him. 'But please, I cannot think that you will always hate me. Let me make you happy man for now, show that I am not only bad. Let me give you goodbye love.'

He looked down at her. 'Whatever you want.'

She undressed methodically, tidily folding her clothes and stacking them on the bedside table that the management had laid out with magazines, condoms, and devices. Naked, she stepped back behind the bloated bed to him and gently pulled his head down to hers to kiss.

'I am so sorry.'

She led him to the bed, insisting that he let her undress him, kissing the skin she bared.

'I am your sorry servant.'

Phoney, he thought, watching her. As phoney as this grotesque room, as the whole hotel with its ocean-liner façade. As the baby.

She lay back and he slipped astride her. Her hand found the control panel and started the bed in slow revolution.

'You want?' she asked. 'For goodbye love?'

'No – I don't want.'

She clicked the switch back. 'Tonight all you want is happen.'

Phoney.

But as he felt the heat of her body, saw her twist and clutch and cry as he had never seen her before, he began to wonder.

Afterwards he watched her face: eyes closed; breathing light and even. He could see no deception in it. But then he had noticed none before.

He glanced out of the window at the ramshackle landscape beyond, full moon rising above the horizon, shining beige through the Tokyo air.

Then he rested his head back on the pillow. The events of the day soon began to draw him into drowsiness. His breathing became slower and more regular. Slowly his consciousness began to drift.

He did not see Keiko's eyes as they blinked open, fixed on his face.

Chapter Eleven

The first thing that Daniel saw when he woke was Keiko, still naked, filling a mug with water from the small clinical sink built into the corner. She crossed to the circular bed, climbed on top of him, gently prised open his lips and raised the mug for him to drink.

'Where do you go now?'

'To the airport.'

'I come also?'

'No, I think I'd better go alone.'

She clambered off him and began to dress, unfolding her clothes and pulling them over her body in a methodical, sexless way. He climbed out of the bed and crossed to the window. Outside the sun was shining, the pavements almost dry. He reached up to the curtain rail.

'What is that?' she asked.

'The door key.' He had thought she was not looking.

'Why do you put it there?'

'It's safer.'

She said nothing.

He washed, and dressed as quickly as he could. His hand felt inside the jacket pocket to check that the passport and ticket were there. He turned to Keiko, standing quite still by the bed.

'There's not much time.' He took her by the shoulders. 'It's best we say goodbye here – in private.' He kissed her lips. She gave no response. It was like kissing something not alive. He felt he should say something to soothe her. 'I'm sorry it ended like this. I won't forget you.'

It sounded wrong.

She looked to the ground. He unlocked the door – the key did not seem to fit, turning with difficulty – and hurried down the corridor, past the fake lifebelts, out into the open air.

He squinted in the bright light and stood for a moment, trying to rid himself of a sensation of griminess. After all, he told himself, it was she who had brought him into all this trouble. For all he knew, she might still be scheming against him.

He began walking, soon reaching a shopping area busy with people eagerly stocking up with new clothes and food. Several times he glanced behind him to find out if he was being followed. The pavement was too crowded to see far.

He saw the entrance to a subway station. Recognizing the insignia, he realized that he was only a few stops down the line from Takasago. He hurried down the stairway, against the current of passengers, and made his way through to the ticket machines.

His eyes scoured the subway map for Takasago, one of the few pieces of Japanese writing that held any meaning for him. The map told him the price: one hundred and eighty yen. He slotted coins into a machine and pressed the button.

'You must not go there – it is dangerous.'

Keiko was standing just a few feet behind him, watching.

'What on earth are you doing here?' he demanded.

'I follow you.'

'Yes, but why?'

'You think I am your enemy.'

'But that's not true.'

'No – I know so. And now you go to Takasago.'

She had seen him buying the ticket, so there was no point in denying it. 'Yes, I have to get the slides.'

'But my father may be there. You do not know what he will do to you.'

'He won't get the chance.'

She took the lapel of his jacket and gave it a sharp tug, as if trying to force him to see things her way. 'You are wrong. Crazy wrong.'

'I can't just leave these things behind. They're a year's work.'

'Then I come with you.'

'Why can't you just leave me in peace?' he said angrily. 'I can sort this out myself.'

'No, quite wrong. I must come.'

'Don't you think you've done enough already?'

'You think so? And so now I must help.'

'No.' He hurried through the ticket barrier to the platform. He could hear her footsteps, three paces behind.

'I told you – you mustn't come.'

'You cannot stop me.'

From the look in her eyes he saw she was not going to give in. He would just have to try and make sure he was well ahead of her when they reached the apartment.

'All right. But you stay away from the actual building. I'll go up alone. All right?'

She said nothing.

From Takasago station he chose a route through the main shopping streets – there was safety in crowds. They were lively with housewives wheeling bicycles, clutching baskets, and chattering to one another as if they had been shuttered in their houses for weeks.

As they approached his street, he walked more slowly,

peering further ahead. There was no sign of the Haradas or their car. The road was empty of people or traffic. Until they reached the level crossing. Out of a side street stepped the all too familiar figure of Samuel Echtbein.

'So you're back, huh? Or did you just want a last taste of Japanese girl before you moved on.'

'There's no time to explain now,' said Daniel hurriedly. 'I've found out a few things about your precious country since we last met – enough to forget your advice.' He turned to move on. Keiko had already marched ahead.

'Oh no you don't.' Echtbein caught him with the hook of his stick. 'You've a lot of unfinished business here. There's people who want to speak with you.'

'There's no time. Take my word for it – they're not good people to speak with.'

Echtbein waved his hand sternly. 'I'm afraid that's not good enough. You're not leaving my sight until I know exactly what's been going on between you and the Haradas, and until I'm satisfied with your behaviour.'

His voice was tinny but nevertheless piercingly audible. Daniel glanced anxiously up at the windows of the apartment. He saw no sign of life. He pushed away Echtbein's stick.

'Why don't you mind your own business and stop prying into other people's lives?'

'There's a law in this country, don't forget,' snapped Echtbein, close behind. 'You'll find that you can't just ride roughshod through people's homes, breaking their families.'

They were by the apartment; Keiko was already tripping up the stairway. Daniel whispered urgently for her to stop, but she hurried up towards the door, hanging open in the breeze.

He felt the sinking sensation of one who sees all slipping

gently outside his control. For an instant he considered making a run for it. But there was no indication that the Haradas were actually in the building. He stopped to watch.

Echtbein poked him with his stick. 'Maybe back in England you can get away with behaving as you have. But you're not in England now.'

'Can't you shut up?' whispered Daniel urgently.

'I will not,' replied Echtbein, with fresh outrage.

'You don't know what's going on here.'

'I know enough to see that you are up to no good.'

His three sons had been following. They stared up at them, solemnly watching the dispute.

'They could be in there – Keiko's family.'

'And you're scared of meeting with them, huh? I can guess why.'

Daniel's next comment was cut short by the sound of the window opening above them. Keiko leant out, her face dulled as if from shock.

'Are they up there?' Daniel called out.

She shook her head. 'No. Myself alone. But terrible.'

With Echtbein clattering behind him, Daniel began to make his way up the stairs. Stopping short of the top, he peered round the corner. Keiko was quite alone, just as she had said. But this was not what struck Daniel.

The place was wrecked: desk and cupboards over-turned; floor littered with books, cutlery, whisky bottles, bowls, and torn clothes. Literally strewn amongst the destruction were hundred upon hundred of tiny card-board squares – his slide collection. Daniel stared, trying to take in what had happened.

'I do not know he does this,' murmured Keiko. 'It must be last night.'

Daniel stepped into the room, picking his way through the debris.

'What's been going on?' Even Echtbein was subdued by the sight. Only his sons were unaffected. They filed past him to begin sifting through the broken objects, examining.

Daniel picked up a lens, the glass shattered. 'I told you that these people were up to no good,' he said, speaking very slowly, 'although I never thought they'd do something quite like this.'

Echtbein frowned. 'But that's crazy – they built it all.'

'It is my father,' said Keiko, looking to the ground. 'He is too angry.'

Echtbein picked up a part of a shattered plate. 'But you're not sure – I mean it's not proven. And a nice guy like that. I say it's more likely to have been burglars. Even some westerner – someone you knew Dan, someone with a grudge.'

'As if it matters what you think.' Daniel picked out a plastic bag, undamaged, and began scooping the slides into it. Keiko knelt down to help him.

'The police'll have to be called in, that's for sure,' resumed Echtbein. 'They'll have everybody sit down and give their versions of what happened here. They'll sort it out. In fact, if I were you, I wouldn't rearrange things – that's all evidence.' He called out to his sons, who abruptly stopped their sifting.

Daniel ignored him – his bag was already almost full. While Echtbein searched for a telephone to call the police, he scoured the debris for more slides. Many were torn, the cardboard frames ripped. He took them all, in the hope that the photographs themselves would be undamaged.

A second bag of slides was almost filled and Echtbein still had not found the telephone, when Keiko abruptly stopped picking through the wreckage. She sat up, quite still.

'What is it?'

'Outside – I hear.'

He heard it too – a car door slamming. He jumped up to the window. Below was a black car-roof, overlong.

'Something up?' demanded Echtbein.

'My family come,' said Keiko.

'All the better. Now we can sit down and sort all this out.'

Daniel was already running through the carnage to the window on the far side. Nobody in sight. A few feet beneath the window was a narrow ledge, just wide enough to help him clamber down. He began to lower himself out. His feet were hanging in the air, feeling for solid support, when he saw Echtbein reaching down to grasp his arm.

'I'm not having you run out again.'

'For Christ's sake let go.'

Echtbein clutched all the harder. 'This has gotta be settled.'

'They're not reasonable people.'

Daniel heard urgent footsteps on the stairway.

'Lock the door – lock it,' he shouted to Keiko. She froze, as if baffled. Despite the confusion, at that instant the thought occurred to Daniel: had she somehow warned them he would be there?

He tried to throw Echtbein back. But, hanging out of the window as he was, it was almost impossible to muster any force. Echtbein's grip on his arm was intact at the moment when Keiko's father and brothers burst into the room.

Echtbein shouted out to them – some explanation – but the words were lost in the noise of their entry. Had his message been heard, it might have saved him; might have helped them realize that he was preventing Daniel from escaping, not assisting him down.

As it was, Masayuki had no doubts in his mind. Without any hesitation he plucked up Echtbein's stick from the ground and used it to strike the man's head. There was an ugly squawk of pain. The grip on Daniel's shoulder relaxed and his feet found the ledge. He jumped down to the ground.

Shouts above. Daniel pulled himself to his feet without looking up. In his mind he imagined Keiko shouting out, her finger pointing after him.

He began running. Around him was a chanting of voices, as if to encourage him on.

'Hurro hurro *Gaijin san*,' they shouted — a whole chorus, leaning out of school windows, empty of malice, only triumphant at having seen a foreigner. '*Gaijin san, Gaijin san.*'

He was nearing the level crossing now, nearing the crowds. He chanced a look behind him and saw the two brothers tearing after him, a few yards back, their father behind them, clutching Echtbein's stick. Then Keiko.

He hurried over the crossing, into open ground. Ahead were a group of housewives. They drew back, alarmed by the sight of a foreigner running so wildly. Still they were blocking the way. Daniel struck a bicycle, crashing to a halt on the tarmac. But he would be safe now, amongst the housewives.

He tried to pull himself up, only to have the breath knocked from him by a sudden blow to his ribs. Through senses hazy with pain, he heard the frightened shrieks of the housewives, saw Masayuki's face leering down at him.

Two pairs of arms hauled him up and threw him against

a wall. Mr Harada's face was close in front of his eyes, the stick ready in his hands. Keiko was nowhere to be seen.

'It is time for you,' barked her father. 'You are too much for us – too much the hippy, the man with no sight.'

The air was filled with the monotone shrieking of the warning siren of the crossing.

'I meant no harm.'

The stick rose up into the air in front of his eyes. The grip on his shoulders ceased and on his chest he felt the heavy pain of the first blow. He slipped down, but was hauled back into place.

'You're wrong – I didn't realize.'

Another blow – this time to the neck, and sharper. The buildings and faces in front of him began to swim into greyness. But still he saw clearly enough to make out the stick as it rose up for the third time. This blow he was sure would strike his skull and would be the last. He felt the grip on his shoulders relax. He closed his eyes.

The pain did not come. He waited, sensing the moment again and again. Nothing.

He opened his eyes. His vision was poor, but clear enough to see that there was nobody in front of him, nor at the sides. They had gone.

Somewhere there was shouting. As his eyes began to focus more clearly, they picked out the small figure in the distance on the railway crossing, half standing, half crouched. One leg was stiff, as if glued to the track.

There was a familiarity to the scene. Daniel watched without surprise, with a vague sense of having seen it before, as the three larger figures ran out towards the other, one of them hurling away a stick as he went. The barriers began their slow descent.

He heard the rumble of the train, then saw it cascade

towards the crossing. They had almost reached the barriers. The machine was travelling too fast and the brakes screeched ineffectually. The three figures sprang back.

Daniel Thayne sat on the steps of the temple. Around him was falling a thin veil of rain.

The police questions were over. He could leave the country. In fact his interrogators had made it more than clear that they did not expect him or want him to stay.

But his thoughts were not of them, nor even of where he might go next. They were of Keiko, and had been of Keiko for some days.

It was not the way she had looked that he remembered most − the way she had been broken by the machine. Rather it was the way both her feet had been unhurt. It was almost as if she had not, as had been claimed, been caught in the line. It was almost as if she had not been trapped at all.

He stared out through the veil of rain.